## "I really should g[o...]"

"How many times are you going to say that?" Hudson asked.

"Until I convince myself to follow through, I guess."

"I like you, Amanda. I also want you. I guess that's no big surprise. But maybe it would be better if we didn't go there."

She nodded. "Much wiser."

"Good night, then."

"Yes, good night." She turned, got as far as the door, actually had her hand on the knob when she turned to look at him one more time.

The naked hunger she saw in his eyes did her in. No man had ever looked at her like that, as if she was the last morsel of bread on earth. And Amanda could no more deny her own desire than she could stop breathing.

"Don't look so glum about it. I have to lower my blood pressure, too. We can work on it together."

She brightened. "Could we make it a contest? Whoever lowers their blood pressure the most gets, um…" *Gets to kiss the other one senseless.*

# THE MILLIONAIRE NEXT DOOR
## Kara Lennox

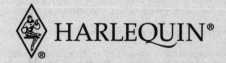

HARLEQUIN®

TORONTO • NEW YORK • LONDON
AMSTERDAM • PARIS • SYDNEY • HAMBURG
STOCKHOLM • ATHENS • TOKYO • MILAN • MADRID
PRAGUE • WARSAW • BUDAPEST • AUCKLAND

ISBN 0-373-16990-6

THE MILLIONAIRE NEXT DOOR

Copyright © 2003 by Karen Leabo.

This edition published by arrangement with Harlequin Books S.A.

® and TM are trademarks of the publisher. Trademarks indicated with
® are registered in the United States Patent and Trademark Office, the
Canadian Trade Marks Office and in other countries.

Visit us at www.eHarlequin.com

**Printed in U.S.A.**

## ABOUT THE AUTHOR

Texas native Kara Lennox has been an art director, typesetter, advertising copywriter, textbook editor and reporter. She's worked in a boutique, a health club and has conducted telephone surveys. She's been an antiques dealer and briefly ran a clipping service. But no work has made her happier than writing romance novels.

When Kara isn't writing, she indulges in an ever-changing array of weird hobbies, from rock climbing to crystal digging. But her mind is never far from her stories. Just about anything can send her running to her computer to jot down a new idea for some future novel.

## Books by Kara Lennox

Don't miss any of our special offers. Write to us at the following address for information on our newest releases.

Harlequin Reader Service
U.S.: 3010 Walden Ave., P.O. Box 1325, Buffalo, NY 14269
Canadian: P.O. Box 609, Fort Erie, Ont. L2A 5X3

# R~X~

**Name:** Hudson Stack, M.D.
**Diagnosis:** High Blood Pressure

---

**General Instructions:**
- Take a vacation in a small Texas town.
- Spend some quality time with your adorable daughter.
- Learn how to fish.
- Fall head over heels in love with your beautiful blond neighbor.

**Signed:** George Blake Stimson, M.D.

# Prologue

Hudson Stack, M.D., sat in the office of George Blake Stimson, Chief of Surgery at Boston General, his irritation rising as he learned the results of his mandatory physical.

"Your blood pressure is in the red zone," George said, continuing a long harangue. "Your cholesterol is off the charts, your triglycerides are completely out of whack. Your caffeine consumption is three times what it ought to be. Your reflexes are slow, you're sleep deprived, and you're irritable. And no doctor, I don't care how famous or how popular, is going to operate on patients in my hospital when he's falling apart."

"Are you telling me I'm fired?" Hudson asked, alarmed. He'd had these little discussions with George before. Usually the crusty old surgeon warned him to take it easy, eat healthier, get more sleep, that sort of thing.

Hudson had believed his job was secure. He'd recently become the hospital's best public relations tool. Inventing an artificial valve that was going to save millions of lives had put Hudson's name in the medical journals. Saving the mayor's life with an emergency quintuple bypass had put his name in the headlines. Most recently, *Boston Life* magazine had named him "Boston's Hottest Bachelor," ensuring he remain in the public eye far longer than Hudson would have liked.

"Of course you're not fired. Administration would tar and feather me if I did that. But you are going on vacation, starting now."

"I can't," Hudson immediately replied. "I've got two surgeries in the morning and three more—"

"Those surgeries will be reassigned to other surgeons."

"You can't do that."

"I can and will do whatever it takes. Would you want a surgeon in your shape operating on *your* heart?"

"There's nothing wrong with me."

"Your test results speak differently."

Hudson knew that arguing was fruitless. George's word was like God's around here. Hudson could appeal to no one; no one would take his side.

"I suppose I could use a few days off," he finally said, grudgingly. And maybe it was true. He hadn't seen his daughter in a week—at least, not awake. He usually got home long after she was in bed. He would spend a few minutes just looking at Bethany as she slept, reassuring himself that she was fine.

"I'm not talking about a few days," George said. "I want you to take off at least a month. And I want you to get far, far away from Boston and go someplace where nobody knows you. And I want you to learn to fish."

Hudson just sat there, stunned. A month? He couldn't take that long away from his work.

"Hudson, I'm not speaking now as your superior, but as your friend. You're a heart attack waiting to happen. Maybe not this week, or this year, but you're heading in that general direction. I even heard you were seen smoking."

"What snitch told you that?" He smoked two, maybe three cigarettes a day. Smoking gave him an excuse to slip outside, alone, and do nothing for a few minutes.

George rolled his eyes. He handed Hudson a piece of paper with an address and phone number on it. "Ed Hardison and I were in med school together. He lives in Texas. I want you to call him. He'll find a place for you to stay. He has a fishing boat and all the tackle."

This was like some drug-induced nightmare. Texas? In the summer? "You're serious about the fishing?"

"It's the best therapy for stress I can think of," George said with a dreamy look in his eye. "Take your kid. Spend a month or two doing absolutely nothing. After that, you'll have another physical. If you look better then, you can come back to work."

Hudson went straight home, cursing the entire time. He was just angry enough that he was going to call George's bluff. There were probably half a dozen hospitals in the Boston area drooling to have him on staff.

As he waited for an interminable traffic light to change, he checked his cell phone messages. Janey had called with a litany of reminders: have his tux cleaned, have his car serviced, call his aunt on her birthday tomorrow. Oh, and the Heart Association fund-raiser was Friday night.

His mother had called with a similar list—and he *was* planning to take Janey to the fund-raiser, right?

He sighed. He hated black-tie affairs, but they were a necessary evil, he supposed. At least he never had to scrounge for a date. Janey was always available. He probably should just marry her and get it over with. He knew she would say yes if he asked. Lord knew she'd been hinting at it long enough.

Another message was from some radio station that wanted to interview him. He erased that one. The last thing he wanted was more publicity.

The final three messages were from women he'd never heard of who thought they were just what a lonely but rich doctor might need to make his life complete. He made a mental note to have his phone number changed—again.

He parked his Jaguar at the curb and stomped through the front door of his Back Bay brownstone. Though he owned two other houses, he'd bought this one because it was close to the hospital. He'd intended to spend only an occasional night here, when he didn't want to face a long drive home late at night. But he'd found it so convenient, he'd ended up living here full-time.

He headed straight for his home office. But the sound of a little girl's laughter stopped him.

Bethany. Guilt needled his conscience. He really should spend more time with her. Though his mother and mother-in-law took turns caring for Bethany, and they both seemed anxious for the privilege, nothing took the place of a father's love and attention. He set down his briefcase and headed up the stairs to the living room. It was lunchtime. He would eat lunch with Bethany, he decided. Then he would figure out his next move.

He found Bethany sitting on the floor of the living room watching TV. She had spread the sofa cushions all over the Persian rug in some game of pretend, and was now sprawled across them, her thumb in her mouth.

"Bethany!" his mother, Judith, called from the dining room. "Lunch is ready. Come quickly, now, before it gets cold."

Bethany, not seeing Hudson, hopped up and scampered to obey her Grandma Judith. Hudson smiled. His daughter was a well-behaved girl, thanks to the time she spent with her grandmothers, who were already grooming her to be a debutante.

Looking forward to eating lunch with his daughter, Hudson paused to pick up the sofa cushions so his mother wouldn't fuss. Since his housekeeper always prepared too much food, he knew there would be plenty.

"Is Philip eating with us?" he heard Bethany ask from the dining room. Philip was Judith's chauffeur.

"Bethany, dear, Philip is a servant. Now that you're a young lady, you don't eat with the servants."

Hudson cringed. He was all for Bethany growing up into a refined young lady, but he didn't condone snobbery. His mother, however, had been raised in a different era, and she couldn't be talked out of her opinions about class and station.

"But I like Philip," Bethany argued. "When he takes me to school, I tell everybody he's my daddy."

Hudson froze, horrified.

"Now, Bethany," Judith said in a very reasonable tone, though her voice shook, "we've talked about this. Philip is a very nice man, and you should always be kind to him. But he is not your father."

Hudson didn't think, he just acted. He waltzed into the room, a smile pasted on his face.

Bethany stared at him in surprise. "Daddy!"

At least she recognized him. "Good news," he announced. "Bethany and I are going on a father-daughter vacation. We're going to learn to fish."

## Chapter One

"Look, Daddy, a cowboy!" Bethany squealed.

Hudson had just pulled his rental car into a space on the Cottonwood, Texas, town square. Sure enough, a wiry man wearing faded Wrangler jeans, pointy-toed boots and a white cowboy hat climbed out of the truck next to their car. He saw them, smiled and tipped his hat before going on about his business.

Bethany stared at him in rapt fascination, and kept right on staring as she climbed out of the rental car. Everything delighted her.

He took her hand and they walked into Tri-County Realty, which George's friend Ed Hardison had recommended. A woman in her fifties with a bleach-blond beehive and thin, penciled eyebrows sat behind a desk talking on the phone. She made eye contact with Hudson and held up a finger to indicate she'd be with him in a minute.

Hudson nodded, his irritation rising. He'd been looking forward to escaping all the attention he'd been receiving in Boston, but that didn't mean he wanted to be ignored.

He wandered over to a bulletin board that featured

photographs of various properties for sale and for rent. Bethany climbed up on a chair to study the photos with him.

"I want to live here, Daddy," she said, pointing to the most opulent home on the board, a huge mansion on the lake. The asking price was almost a million dollars, which seemed cheap to Hudson. In Boston a property like that would cost three or four times as much.

"That one's for sale, not for rent," he explained, though he had no idea if Bethany understood the difference. "When the nice lady gets off the phone, we'll see everything that's available."

"Margie never gets off the phone," a voice from an interior office called out. The voice was brisk, but with a honey-edged Southern accent.

Intrigued, Hudson followed the sound of the voice through a doorway, finding himself in a large, well-appointed office with a view of the town square. But the woman who worked here apparently didn't want to take advantage of the view. She had her desk turned so she had her back to the window, and the shades were drawn.

Her walls were covered with plaques—top seller for her company, at least three years running. Million Dollar Club. An award from the chamber of commerce for Cottonwood's Ambassador of the Year. Other spots on the wall were filled with framed letters from grateful clients. Hudson recognized the name of a country-western singer and a former lieutenant governor.

The woman stood up and held out her hand, shaking

his with a firm grip that made him fear for his surgeon's hands. It seemed odd that such a delicate hand could wield so much strength. "Nice to meet you. I'm Amanda Dewhurst."

"Hudson. Stack." He held his breath, waiting for the inevitable reaction. Back home, if someone didn't instantly recognize him, they at least knew his name. *Oh, you're that bachelor doctor guy.* At which point they would wax eloquent about their uncle's heart disease or try to set him up with a little sister.

He was tired of dealing with that. He didn't want anyone bothering him, inviting him to parties, interviewing him for the paper or trying to seduce him. He just wanted to be a guy on vacation with his daughter. He didn't hold out much hope. His notoriety as a surgeon might not extend this far from Boston, but everyone knew who the Boston Stacks were. They were right up there with the Kennedys. For generations, Stacks had been senators, judges, philanthropists and tycoons.

Amazingly, Amanda didn't bat an eye. "Pleased to meet you." She turned a dazzling smile on Bethany. "Hi, sugar. What's your name? Would you like a piece of candy?" Amanda looked up at Hudson. "Can she have a piece of candy?"

"I don't eat candy," Bethany said primly. "It rots your teeth."

"So it does," Amanda replied, her composure unshaken. "How about an apple?"

A tiny refrigerator sat behind Amanda's desk. When she opened it, he caught a glimpse of can after can of

Slimfast—and one red apple. She grabbed the apple and brought it out, offering it to Bethany.

Bethany accepted the apple, thanked Amanda, then didn't eat it. She seemed enthralled with the beautiful office—and with Amanda herself, whom Hudson confessed wasn't bad to look at. She was petite, with silver-blond hair and a pixie face. Her hair was unfortunately pulled into a tight twist, piquing Hudson's curiosity. How long was it?

She wore a red skirt with a sheer white blouse and a black patent-leather belt at her slim waist. Her nails were shiny red and salon-fresh, her complexion fair and flawless, her lips skillfully painted. She was about as well put together as any woman he'd ever seen, and he'd spent his whole life around females with wealth and style.

The surprise was finding her in this backwater town.

"What can I do for you this fine spring day?" she asked.

"We're looking for a furnished house to rent. Ed Hardison said I should go through Tri-County."

Amanda smiled. "You're friends of the Hardisons? Such nice people," she went on without waiting for an answer. "I sold Allison Hardison's house a few months ago when she and Jeff got married. What kind of house are you looking for?"

"We want a house with a lake," Bethany said.

Amanda beamed. "We have some lovely lakefront homes available. Are you new to the area?"

"Just visiting," Hudson said. "We'll only be here a month. We're looking for a furnished rental."

Amanda's smile faltered. "Oh."

"Is that a problem?"

"It's just that most of the rentals require at least a six-month lease. But that's okay. I can find something. Let me check our listings."

"We want the big house—out there," Bethany said, pointing to the outer office.

Amanda got a dreamy look in her eye. "You must mean the Clooney place. It's the prettiest house on the lake. Unfortunately, it's not for rent."

Hudson almost agreed to buy it. It was hard for him to deny his daughter anything. But the house probably wouldn't come with furniture, and he didn't want to spend his whole vacation buying stuff for a house he would occupy for a few weeks, tops.

"I'm sure we can find something else," he said.

Amanda's pretty hands flew over her computer keyboard in a curiously sensual way. Hudson found himself staring at those hands, and the way her breasts jiggled ever so slightly with the enthusiasm she put into the typing. That sheer blouse revealed a lacy camisole underneath.

She called up property after property on the computer, rejecting each one for one reason or another. Some weren't furnished. Some wouldn't take children. Some were already rented.

"You don't have any pets, do you?" Amanda asked.

"No," Hudson said. Thank God.

"But I'm going to get a pony," Bethany said hopefully.

Amanda pored over her listings, but she couldn't locate a single rental house on the lake that didn't have some barrier to Hudson renting it. He could have offered more money. Every fussy landlord had his price. But he didn't want to call attention to his financial status. He was playing the part of an average guy, and an average guy didn't have money to burn.

"I have several rentals in town," Amanda said hopefully. "There's a beautiful Victorian right on the square."

"I want to be on the water," Hudson said firmly. "I'm here to fish."

"What about the Skillman cabin?" Margie called from the reception area.

Amanda's face stiffened. "I don't think you'd be interested in that one."

"Why not?" Hudson asked.

"It's small, for one thing."

"There's just the two of us."

"And I'm little so I don't take up much room," Bethany added.

"It's furnished," Margie called.

"Margie, do you want to come in here and work with Mr. Stack?" Amanda asked, though the teasing tone in her voice softened the sarcasm. "I could take a coffee break."

"Well, I'm just trying to help. Jeez."

"So what about this cabin?" Hudson asked. "Do you have a picture of it?"

Amanda sighed. "Yes, somewhere. It's not in the computer yet. I'm afraid it doesn't have much curb appeal. It's rather…rustic."

Bethany climbed up in her chair and leaned over

the desk, to better observe what Amanda was doing. "What does rustic mean, Daddy?"

"It means, um, old-fashioned and not very luxurious."

"Like Grandma Ruth's apartment?"

"Sort of." Hudson's mother-in-law lived in an old brownstone, with fashionably worn Oriental rugs, creaking wood floors, 1960s appliances and a rotary telephone. He supposed some people would consider that rustic. Ruth Hanover had enough money to buy any modern luxury she wanted, but she insisted nothing worthwhile had been manufactured in the past thirty years.

Finally Amanda produced a creased photo of a no-frills A-frame log cabin, not very big. But it did have a dock.

"Does it have electricity and running water?" Hudson asked.

"Sometimes. I really don't think—"

"It's like Abe Lincoln's house!" Bethany exclaimed. "I want to live there, Daddy."

Well, that cinched it. "Can we go see it?"

"Okay," Amanda replied without much enthusiasm.

AMANDA WISHED Margie had kept her suggestions to herself. She didn't want to rent out the Skillman cabin, because it happened to be next door to her own. Every single renter who'd leased the cabin had been noisy, annoying and low class. The last tenant had thrown loud parties and trashed the place, and the Skillmans hadn't bothered to clean it up. Now it was empty, and Amanda preferred it that way.

Still, Hudson didn't appear to be rowdy, though it was always hard to tell on a first meeting. He was good-looking, that was for sure. Though he was at least in his mid-thirties, his body had a youthful vigor, all lean muscle and smooth coordination. His hair was short and dark, but she could tell it had some natural curl to it. He had a square jaw, square shoulders and square hands—not much softness to him.

She liked that.

His East Coast accent called to mind Kennedys and Rockefellers. But somehow she doubted he fell into that category, or he'd be vacationing in Martha's Vineyard or some such place. Cottonwood's reputation as a fishing and boating mecca was growing, and it drew visitors from Dallas and Houston. But Boston?

The fact Hudson was even considering the rundown Skillman cabin meant he probably didn't have a lot of money. Still, a commission was a commission. Maybe he'd like it here and decide to stay, and she'd sell him a house.

At any rate, she wasn't going to let Mary Jo Dickens get him. Mary Jo was vying with Amanda for first place in sales this month, and Amanda didn't like it one bit. Amanda had boasted top sales every month for four years, and she intended to maintain her streak. Even a small commission might be enough to edge Mary Jo ahead of Amanda.

She unlocked the doors of her silver Lincoln with a press of a button on her key chain.

"This is a pretty car," Bethany said when they were all settled into the soft leather seats.

"Thank you," Amanda said. The payments were eating her alive, but she firmly believed a luxurious car put her clients in the mood to buy. "So what brings you to Cottonwood?"

"Daddy got fired," Bethany announced, as if it were something to be proud of.

Alarm bells went off in Amanda's mind. If Mr. Stack didn't have a job, how was he going to pay for even a small rental house? Lakefront property wasn't cheap, not even the Skillman cabin.

"Let's call it a leave of absence, Bethany," Hudson said quickly. "A long-overdue vacation, really."

"And what sort of work do you do?"

She wasn't sure, but she thought he tensed at the question. And he didn't answer right away. Finally he said, "I work at a hospital."

She observed him from the corner of her eye. His clothes, while a bit rumpled, appeared to be quality made. He had a good haircut and nice teeth that had probably seen braces. Nice eyes, too, a very deep, sincere brown.

"Are you a doctor?" she finally asked when he offered no more details.

Again, that slight tension. "I do repair work."

Was he lying? Was he an escaped convict, or a noncustodial dad who'd kidnapped his daughter?

Well, it was none of her business, so long as he could pay the rent. And if he really was a repairman, maybe he could do some work on the Skillman cabin. The owners would probably give him a break on the rent if he did a little patching and painting. She mentioned this possibility to him.

"I'm on vacation," he said. "I plan to relax."

Well, that put her in her place.

"Here it is," she said as she pulled into the gravel driveway. She didn't bother pointing out any of the house's finer points, because there just weren't any. As Hudson wandered through the house, silently observing the ancient appliances and leaky plumbing, the worn carpet and musty odor, he said little.

Bethany, however, was running through the house as if it were a playground.

"Look at this, Daddy!" she exclaimed, pointing to a sleeping loft. The only access was by ladder. "Can I sleep up here, Daddy, please, please? I want that to be my room."

Amanda smiled at the child's enthusiasm. Children had a way of filtering out the unpleasant and focusing on the positives. She remembered some of the places she'd lived as a child. Though they might have been dumps, her father would always manage to sell her by pointing out the things children loved—a tree with a tire swing, or a patio with a picnic table, or a nearby creek where they could catch tadpoles. And she could overlook leaky roofs and peeling paint.

Actually, the Skillman cabin was a palace compared to some of the places she'd lived.

HUDSON WAS ON THE VERGE of grabbing his child and running back to Boston. This place was a trash heap! But then he thought about what George would say, and he controlled the urge. He could stand anything for a month.

There was no way to fake this vacation, either. He'd thought about checking into a four-star resort in Florida or California and simply staying out of touch for a month. But he couldn't lie to George, who'd been his mentor for a dozen years. George was convinced Cottonwood was the medicine Hudson needed, and nothing else would do. He wanted Hudson to be bored.

They walked out onto the rickety dock. "Are there fish in this lake?" Hudson asked.

"Oh, loads," Amanda replied.

"Can I catch some goldfish?" Bethany asked.

Amanda laughed. It was a musical, tinkling laugh that seemed to shiver down Hudson's spine. For the first time since he'd met her, Hudson thought he saw through Ms. Super-Efficient Realtor to the real woman beneath. And he liked what he saw.

"No goldfish in Town Lake," she said. "But the pet store on the square has goldfish. That's one pet you can keep in a rental house."

"Who lives in that house?" Bethany asked, pointing to a tidy A-frame home next door to theirs. It was similar in style to theirs, but quite a bit larger—and nicer.

"A fairy princess lives there," Amanda answered in a confidential whisper.

"Really? Where? Where is she?"

"She's standing right here on the dock with you."

"I don't see her."

Amanda laughed again. "I'm only teasing, Bethany. Actually, that's my house."

Hudson's interest in the rental cabin ratcheted up a notch. He'd heard the saying location-location-location, and a desirable neighbor could make the location sweet.

"Can I come visit you?" Bethany asked.

"Anytime you like. Although I'm not home very much."

"Neither is my daddy," Bethany said.

Another twinge of guilt. How long would it take to regain Bethany's trust? Ah, who the hell was he kidding? He'd never had it to begin with. Bethany had been only two years old when Elaine had died in a skiing accident—while skiing with her boyfriend. The shock of her death *and* her infidelity had been too much for Hudson. He'd thrown himself into his work like a demon. Immersed in a complicated surgery, he could forget Elaine and her painful betrayal.

Unfortunately, in forgetting Elaine he'd also neglected the emotional needs of his daughter.

Well, he intended to make up for his shortcomings as a father. Children were resilient and forgiving. He would get back in Bethany's good graces if it killed him. And if she wanted to live in this ramshackle cabin and sleep in a loft and visit the fairy princess next door, so be it.

"I'll take the cabin," he said abruptly.

"Really?" Amanda seemed surprised. "I haven't even told you how much it is."

"How much is it?"

"Seven hundred."

"A week?"

She laughed. "A month."

Holy cow, that was cheap. He'd never lived in a place that cost so little. ''That's fine.''

They returned to the Tri-County rental office, where Hudson was required to fill out an application, though Amanda assured him it was only a formality. His pen hovered over the space marked ''Occupation.'' He'd misled Amanda, but he couldn't make himself lie on paper. He wrote in ''doctor'' very quickly and hoped no one would read it.

He wrote out a check for one month's rent plus a security deposit. It had been so long since he'd actually written a check, he had to stop and think about it. He had a business manager who handled all of his bills. When he did have to deal with financial things, he used credit cards.

When he'd hastily packed for this trip, he'd grabbed his old checkbook from a desk drawer, realizing not everyone accepted credit cards, especially out in the sticks. He congratulated himself for thinking ahead.

Amanda took the check and the application, paper-clipped them together, and stuck them in a folder on her fanatically neat desk.

''Thanks for helping me out,'' he said as he stood.

She stood also and handed him the key to the cabin. ''Thanks for the business. Please let me know if I can help you with anything else. And welcome to the neighborhood.''

He shook her hand again, holding it for a little longer than was necessary.

THE FIRST THING Hudson did upon arriving at his new, temporary home was to locate the yellow pages and hire a cleaning service to give the place a good going-over. Rustic he could handle; filthy he couldn't. With a little prodding, he arranged for a housekeeper from Sharon's Personal Service to come out that afternoon. "If I'm not here, the door will be open." It wasn't as if a thief would want to steal anything here.

Next on the list was groceries. He'd never had to prepare his own food before. At Grubbs Food Mart, which appeared to be the only grocery store in town, he filled his basket with frozen foods, snacks and lunch meats for sandwiches. Bethany made her choices clear. She wanted macaroni and cheese, peanut butter and jelly and something called Lunchables that appeared to be cheese and crackers in a box.

George had told him to eat healthily, but since Hudson couldn't cook, he was severely limited. He bought a few apples, some peaches and, at Bethany's urging, a bag of celery.

"I like it with peanut butter," she announced.

In the cleaning products aisle, he picked up some dishwasher detergent. Wait, did the cabin have a dishwasher? Hell, he didn't think so, now that he thought about it. And laundry, how was he supposed to clean his clothes? How was he supposed to relax if he had to worry about all this stuff?

He was putting his groceries in the trunk when he saw a woman barreling toward him through the small parking lot. Not just any woman, he realized. Amanda Dewhurst.

His momentary pleasure was soon blunted by the fact that she was scowling.

As soon as she reached him, she waved a piece of paper in his face. "Would you mind explaining this?"

He grabbed the paper from her hand, which he now saw was his check. "What's wrong?"

"You know damn well what's wrong."

"You're not going to tell me it bounced, are you?" That was ludicrous. He had thousands of dollars in his ready assets account.

"I put it through Checktronic," she fumed. "The account was closed two years ago!"

"What?" With a sinking feeling, Hudson examined the check more closely. Then he realized the names printed on the check were Hudson and Elaine Stack. He'd grabbed the wrong checkbook. This was the account mainly used by Elaine, and his manager *had* closed it.

He tried to explain the mix-up to Amanda. She listened stoically. "It was an honest mistake," he concluded. "I'll make the check good."

"You can't make a check good on a closed account."

She had a point. Hudson felt his collar growing tighter—then realized his collar was open. "I don't suppose you take credit cards."

Amanda tapped her foot.

With a sigh, Hudson reached into his back pocket and pulled out his wallet. He pulled out all of the cash and counted it into Amanda's hand. It amounted to four hundred thirty dollars and change. "I'll get you the rest tomorrow, okay?"

Amanda studied him, considering.

"I'm good for it. Have a heart. I've got a car full of frozen food that's rapidly melting in this heat."

"All right." She stuck the cash in her briefcase. "But I really need it by tomorrow. I'm ahead of Mary Jo Dickens by twenty dollars, and tomorrow is the last day of the month. If I have to deduct the commission from this rental, I'll lose."

"Lose what?" he asked, bewildered.

"I won't be top seller for May. And if I have to see that trophy sitting on Mary Jo's desk for all of next month, I'll puke."

He recalled all those plaques in her office. Million Dollar Club. Top selling Realtor for the past four years running. Those framed letters of appreciation.

It was on the tip of his tongue to say, "So? What's the big deal about having a trophy on your desk?" But then Hudson realized it was a big deal for Amanda. She was as serious and committed about her job as he was about his.

Tomorrow some other doctor would be doing *his* surgery, and he didn't like that, either.

He smiled. "I'll make it good. Don't worry. You'll beat the pants off this Mary Jo, whoever she is."

Amanda managed a watery smile. Then she turned on her shiny black pumps and walked away.

## Chapter Two

Amanda's face burned as she walked back to her office, and it wasn't just the summer heat. What in God's name had possessed her to tell Hudson Stack about her rivalry with Mary Jo Dickens?

"Hey, what's with you?" Margie asked the minute Amanda walked through the door. "You look like a herd of demons is chasing you. Is Mary Jo hassling you again?"

Amanda set her things on one of the plush client chairs and sank into the other one. For once, she didn't feel like rushing back to her office to generate new leads or update her contact list.

"It's not Mary Jo, not this time," Amanda said. "It's me. I just chased down Hudson Stack in the street and gave him hell for writing me a bad check."

"Good for you. He could go to jail for that."

"Except that...I harangued him in front of his little girl. And maybe he did intentionally try to defraud me, but maybe it was an honest mistake. And if it was, I've alienated him permanently. And he's friends with Ed Hardison. You know what'll happen to my business if Ed tells people I'm a harpy?"

"You'll never sell another house," Margie added, deadpan, "and you'll have to move out of town and go into another line of work. Maybe change your name. Go into the witness protection program."

"I think you're making fun of me," Amanda said suspiciously.

"Oh, honey, you're just too damn hard on yourself. No one can be sweet 24/7. So, you lost your temper. You got a little flustered. Who wouldn't, dealing with that guy?"

"What do you mean?"

"I don't know if you noticed, but he's quite the studmuffin." Margie fanned herself with the *Cottonwood Conversation,* the town's weekly newspaper.

Amanda had noticed, all right. Even as she'd been yelling at him, her eyes had been focused on things they shouldn't have been—like the worn places on his jeans, and that little tuft of chest hair peeking out over the top button of his shirt.

"I didn't just yell at him for the check," Amanda confessed. "I also told him about how Mary Jo was going to beat me this month in sales. As if that justified my turning his bad check into a federal case."

Margie had the nerve to laugh. "Boy, you really are bent out of shape. Does it matter so much if she beats you one month?"

"Yes! I mean, no, except that it's not just this month. She's been nipping at my heels all year. If I'm not careful, she'll take my title away."

"And would *that* be so bad? I mean, jeez, Amanda, you've been top seller four out of the past five years. The whole idea of these awards is to inspire agents to work harder and make more money for themselves and the company. Obviously, Mary Jo's inspired, and the competition has helped both of you. And you're already doing better than you did last year. The company's doing great. It's a win-win situation, and that little trophy on your desk, and the plaques on your wall—they're just dumb pieces of wood and brass.''

Amanda stifled a gasp. "Margie, they're not dumb.''

"I'm sorry, kiddo. I didn't mean to minimize your accomplishments. I'm just saying, get some perspective.''

Amanda sighed again. "I can't help it. I just get crazy at the idea of Mary Jo beating me. If it was Hank or Emily, it wouldn't bother me so much. But Mary Jo? She just got her license last year!''

"And how do you think Emily felt when you came along? She was the queen of the Top Seller trophies and plaques before you, and the ink on your license was still wet the first time you beat her.''

Amanda had to think back. Had she been like Mary Jo? God, she hoped not. Amanda was ambitious, but she was ethical. She'd never snooped in other agents' appointment books, stolen a list of contacts or slept with potential clients. Mary Jo had.

"Does Emily hate me?" Amanda asked.

"No, of course not! Her sales overall have gone up since you've been onboard. She has a healthy rivalry with you and with Mary Jo. You, on the other hand…''

"Just stepped over the line. I know.'' Amanda stood. "Okay, I'm turning over a new leaf. Healthy rivalry. Team player. No more sniping about Mary Jo, the witch, behind her back.''

''Ix-nay, here comes the itch-way now.'' Margie gathered up a handful of pink message slips. ''These came in for you while you were gone.''

The door opened and Mary Jo swept in, all five feet, ten inches of her. She had a model's slender hips and legs, but not the flat chest. In fact, her double-Ds challenged whatever blouse she wore, though she always managed to look stylish. Her midnight hair hung straight as water, almost to her waist, shimmering even in the artificial light of the office.

She came from a rich family in Tyler. She had a college degree in marketing, but it was her finishing-school sheen that Amanda secretly envied. Mary Jo had a natural confidence, an ability to talk about anything with anybody. And though she was always decently dressed, her sexuality billowed out from her in clouds, like cheap perfume did on other women.

In a crowded room, like a chamber of commerce meeting, people just naturally gravitated toward Mary Jo, whereas Amanda usually had to initiate contact with people.

''I just showed someone the Clooney mansion,'' Mary Jo said exuberantly. ''They spent almost an hour there. I think they might make an offer!'' She addressed the comment to both women, but she looked at Amanda.

If Mary Jo sold the Clooney mansion, she would shoot ahead of Amanda and would probably be uncatchable.

Damn.

"Good for you," Amanda forced herself to say, pasting on a smile. "It would be a plum for the whole company if one of us could sell that puppy."

"Keep your fingers crossed. Do any good business today, Amanda?"

"Nothing to speak of."

"Well, cheer up. The day's not over." With that she breezed past Amanda toward her own office, grabbing her phone messages on the way.

Amanda bit her tongue. She wanted to say something nasty. That gloating, patronizing bimbo! But the new leaf, and all.

"I'll be in my office," Amanda grated out. She picked up her things and shut herself off from the rest of the world. Maybe she'd have something interesting in her e-mail inbox.

The next time she came up for air, it was eight o'clock and starting to get dark. Her stomach was a gaping cavern of emptiness. She hadn't eaten since she'd wolfed down a bagel for breakfast.

She reached behind her to the refrigerator to grab a Slimfast. But the sudden movement made her head spin, and she realized she needed to eat a real meal before she passed out. She grabbed a couple of real estate magazines—she wanted to draft some new ads, and she needed inspiration. She stuffed them in her briefcase for later, then headed out.

Amanda always felt a rush of pleasure when she drove up to her house on the lake. She'd bought it last year—her very first home. It wasn't grand, as lake houses went, just a modest two-bedroom A-frame. But it was clean—most of the time—and snug. She hadn't needed to do any work on it, and she'd hardly changed a thing except to hang a few pictures.

The important thing was that it was hers, and no one could take it away from her—unless she failed to make her house payments. That possibility was never far from her thoughts. Though she'd had no trouble qualifying for the loan based on her previous three years' income, the real estate business was iffy. One turn of the economic roulette wheel and her income could disappear.

That was why she stockpiled so much. Though her banker urged her to invest in a diverse portfolio, she was content to keep her cash in a money-market fund, where it was readily available for any emergency. She had enough to see her through a whole year, should something happen to her income.

But that didn't stop her from worrying.

She was just a worrier. That was her nature, and there was nothing she could do about it.

And speaking of worrying, what was that taped to her front door?

Instead of entering her house through the garage door, Amanda walked around to the front and up the stairs to her porch. A fat envelope with her name on it was taped to the door. She pulled it off and opened it. It was full of cash—and a note.

She read the note and smiled. Hudson Stack had made good on his check. All that worry for nothing— this time. Maybe she would keep her little desk trophy another month after all.

Her pleasure over this small victory was blunted when she saw what a mess the kitchen was. Her brother, Mick, had obviously been home, had dinner, then left again. The empty pizza box and cardboard had been left on the counter; her microwave was covered in melted cheese; and the greasy plate and leftover crusts had been dumped near, though not in, the sink. An empty pop bottle sat on the counter, mere inches from the pantry door where the trash was stored.

Amanda gritted her teeth and cleaned up the mess. Sometimes she wondered what would happen if she just stopped cleaning up after Mick. Would he even notice? But nagging didn't do any good, nor did threats. He was a twenty-two-year-old boy-man who simply hadn't grown up yet. As soon as she got him through college and he got a job, he would move out on his own and fall in love with some woman, who would reform him.

As she threw a frozen pasta dinner into the microwave, her thoughts returned to Hudson Stack, and she started worrying about something else. What if that cash was all he had? His daughter had said he was out of work. What if he'd needed this cash to live on?

Okay, if this was all he had, he wouldn't have rented a lake house. Unless he'd promised his daughter…

No. She was being ridiculous. Hudson was a grown man, and she had no business worrying about his financial status. If he'd rented a house he couldn't afford, that was his problem. She had her cash up front, and that was all that mattered.

Right?

A PRESSURE AGAINST Hudson's stomach woke him up. He cracked one eye open to a pitch-black room. Bethany was sitting on his rib cage.

"Daddy! Are you awake?"

"I am now." He'd tossed and turned until the wee hours of the morning. It was too quiet here. He missed the white noise of traffic, horns, sirens. He liked the idea that there were people all around him. This house was too isolated. The only nearby neighbor was Amanda Dewhurst, and he'd managed to alienate her.

The quiet had nearly driven him crazy.

"I'm bored," Bethany announced.

Hudson checked the illuminated dial on his watch. It was a little after five o'clock. "Go back to bed. It's too early." It would be six, Boston time. He would already be on his way to the hospital, mentally preparing for his first surgery.

"I can't sleep," Bethany said.

Bethany had never awakened him before. Back home, if she cried in the night or had a bad dream, she went to the live-in housekeeper. She'd been told not to disturb his sleep, because he needed plenty of rest if he was going to stick a scalpel into someone's heart the next day.

Now he had no such excuses. His daughter was his responsibility, totally. It scared him a little.

"Do you want to climb into bed with me?" he asked, a little apprehensively. He wasn't sure that was proper, but maybe it would help her feel more secure if an adult was nearby.

"No. I want you to get up. I'm hungry."

Hudson groaned. "Get a Pop-Tart. They're in the cabinet."

''I can't reach.''

Hudson reached over and turned on the bedside lamp. His daughter stared at him earnestly. He would have to get up—he didn't know what else to do. Maybe he shouldn't have made Bethany take that long nap yesterday.

He set her on her feet, then climbed out of bed and pulled on a pair of jeans.

As he was fixing Bethany a Pop-Tart, he looked out the window and noticed lights on at the house next door. Amanda must be an early riser. He thought about asking her over for coffee. It would be nice to have another adult to talk to. He was going batty here, and he'd been here less than a day.

Then he realized how stupid an idea that was. First, he didn't have any coffee. And even if he did, the cabin didn't have a coffee maker. Second, an attractive woman in his cabin would only make his blood pressure go up. And the objective was to make it go down. He'd brought a cuff with him and he intended to check it often. The moment he got the numbers down to normal, he was heading back to Boston.

Third, Amanda probably wasn't speaking to him. Although he hoped the cash left on her door would lessen her anger with him.

He thought back to the way she'd gone off on him yesterday. Her eyes had sparked fire, and little wisps of blond hair had pulled free of her tight twist, framing her face in a shimmering halo. He'd liked seeing her that way, free of her ultraprofessional real-estate-lady persona. He just wished her anger hadn't been aimed at him.

He thought about her loss of composure and wondered what it meant. Yelling at him about the check he could understand. But that business about Mary Jo Whoever stealing her trophy—that was over the top.

The light upstairs went out, and another came on downstairs. Maybe he could take her *out* for coffee. Did Cottonwood have a Starbucks? He doubted it, but he'd seen something called the Miracle Café that served breakfast all day.

"Are you gonna give me that Pop-Tart or what?" Bethany asked.

Hudson realized he'd been staring at the house, lost in thought. The Pop-Tart had popped up and was cooling off. He plucked it from the toaster, set it on a paper towel, and handed it to Bethany.

"Grandma Ruth says we always have to eat at the table."

"At home, maybe. But we're on vacation."

"What's vacation?"

"You know, a trip. Where we have fun."

"I'm not having fun."

"You didn't like sleeping in the loft?"

"Yeah. But I'm awake now."

"Let's go watch the sunrise."

"Why?"

"Because…because it's pretty. Because that's what people do when they stay in a lake house, I guess."

"What about fishing?"

When Hudson had checked out the house yesterday, he'd seen some fishing equipment in the garage.

"Sure, why not? We'll eat breakfast, get dressed, and by then the sun will be up and we can go fishing."

Thirty minutes later, showered, dressed in old jeans and reasonably well fed with two Pop-Tarts, Hudson was in the garage sorting through a pile of dusty old fishing equipment. He selected what looked like the only two poles that actually had working reels attached. He sort of figured out how the reel worked. He found a tackle box that had an assortment of esoteric things inside, including hooks. He tied a hook onto the end of each line, using surgical knots.

"Piece of cake," he murmured.

All the while, Bethany watched intently, asking him what he was doing each step of the way. He tried to act as if he knew the drill, but he'd never been fishing in his life except for the time he went deep-sea fishing on a yacht. This was a little different.

"The fish bite onto these hooks?" she asked.

"That's right."

"Why do they do that? Are they stupid?"

"No. We have to trick them into biting the hook by putting bait on it."

"What's bait?"

"It's something the fish would like to eat."

"What do fish eat?"

That was a very good question. He rifled through the tackle box, finally coming up with some rather crusty artificial worms. Maybe these would do.

The point wasn't really to catch anything, right? This was an exercise in boredom.

The sun was just coming up as Hudson and Bethany walked out to the end of the rickety dock. Hudson put a rubbery worm on the end of each hook, then pulled out some extra line so the hook would dangle in the water. He gave one pole to Bethany, cautioning her for about the tenth time about being careful of the hook. Then he sat down beside her and put his own hook in the water.

Nothing happened.

"This is nice," he said, trying to convince himself. "Just you and me, doing a little father-daughter bonding."

"Huh?"

"Never mind. Is anything happening with your line?"

"No."

"Mine, neither. But I understand you have to be patient to be a fisherman."

"Fisher*girl*," she corrected him.

Oh, Lord. At four years old, Bethany was a budding feminist. Her grandmother would have a fit. Finally, something to make Hudson smile.

"I'm bored," Bethany said after exactly seven minutes.

"Let's talk to pass the time."

"Talk about what?"

He had no idea what. "What do you like to watch on TV?"

*"Princess Pony."*

"Tell me about that."

"There's a white pony, and she's a princess, and then there's a bad Palomino Queen who wants Princess Pony to go into this cave and never come out."

"That sounds exciting."

"But now I can't watch it because we don't have a TV."

Originally he'd been pleased the cabin didn't have a TV. Bethany watched far too much at home, and the point of a vacation like this was to get outdoors, get some exercise, get healthy. Watching TV wasn't healthy. But it might help Bethany not to die of boredom. Maybe he could compromise, buy a TV and VCR and rent some educational videos or classic children's movies.

"Is anything happening with your line?"

"No."

Eleven minutes had passed.

They tried a different color of worm. They tried an orange lizard. They tried a silver metal fish with spinners on it. The fish were about as interested as Hudson would be at a vegetarian buffet.

"Can we go inside now, Daddy?"

"Not until we catch a fish." He didn't know what he would do with the fish if he caught it, but he didn't like to fail at his endeavors.

AMANDA GULPED DOWN the last bit of her coffee, then strode through the living room and beat on the bedroom door. "Mick? Are you up yet?"

No reply.

She cracked the door open. Mick was sprawled on top of the covers, still fully clothed. It was all Amanda could do not to yank him by the ankles and toss him to the floor.

She'd heard him come home last night—at two in the morning. She'd hoped he was at the university library in Tyler, studying. But seeing him now, she knew she'd been naive. Mick had been out drinking— she'd stake her life on it. It wasn't as if she couldn't recognize the signs. She was very afraid that Mick was his father's son.

Resisting the urge to fit her hands around his neck, she instead shook his shoulder. "Mick. Wake up."

He opened one bleary eye. "Huh?"

"Get your hungover butt out of bed. You have a class this morning."

"Not till nine."

"Get up now, or you'll fall back to sleep."

"Get off my case."

"You think this is on your case? Just wait and see what happens if I ever catch you drinking and driving again."

She left him with that thought. Back in the kitchen, she grabbed her keys and was about to head out the door when she spotted something interesting out the living room window. Hudson and Bethany were sitting on the end of their dock, fishing.

She watched them for a few self-indulgent moments. Her father used to take her fishing when she was a little girl. It was one of her nicest memories of him, nearly obliterated by other, more recent and far less pleasant ones. But now the images came flooding back—baiting hooks with wiggling earthworms, breathlessly watching the float bob up and down as a fish toyed with the bait, feeling the sun beating down on her bare arms.

And listening to her father tell stories. Sometimes he told real stories from his youth. Sometimes he made up fairy tales. And sometimes she couldn't tell the difference. But she didn't care. She just loved to hear him talk. He could weave an interesting tale around the most mundane of events and keep her endlessly entertained.

She wondered what Hudson and Bethany were talking about.

As she watched them a bit longer, she realized they weren't catching anything, not even little perch or sunfish. The longer she watched, the more she realized they hadn't a clue about what they were doing. They didn't even know how to cast!

It's none of your business, she reminded herself. Fishing was very personal. Maybe this was the technique that worked for Hudson.

She had to get to work, anyway. She had an appointment in a couple of hours with Clea Marsden about selling her rental property.    But she could go over and thank Hudson for leaving her the cash. And she could give him a few pointers on fishing. It had been years since she'd dipped a hook in the water, but she hadn't forgotten how.

Yes, that was the polite thing to do. She would have to live next to Hudson for a month. Might as well try to be on good terms with him. Besides, what if he really needed the fish to supplement his groceries?

Her mind made up, she marched next door, then tiptoed down the dock. If there were any fish around, she didn't want to scare them.

''Good morning,'' she whispered.

Hudson jumped a good six inches, and Bethany

peered over her shoulder. "Why are you whispering?" she asked.

"So I don't scare the fish," she explained.

"The fish are underwater," Bethany said patiently. "They can't hear us."

"Oh, but they can," Amanda assured her. Then she looked at Hudson, who appeared touchably rumpled and unshaven. Normally she didn't care for that unshaven look, but on Hudson it worked. He wore a pair of jeans even more faded than the ones he'd had on yesterday, and a Harvard T-shirt.

Harvard? "Your alma mater?" she asked, pointing to the shirt.

He looked down at it. "This? Someone gave it to me."

"Oh. Well, anyway, I wanted to thank you for making good on the check."

"I told you I would."

"I know, but I've learned not to trust people when they say things like that. So many don't live up to their word. I appreciate that you did, and I'm sorry I lost my temper yesterday."

He smiled. "It's forgotten."

"So, you're fishing, huh?"

"Yup."

"What are you using for bait?" She didn't see a bait bucket anywhere.

"Right now? Some little wooden fish we found in the tackle box."

Ye gods! No wonder they hadn't caught anything. You couldn't use plastic worms or plugs or other artificial lures for bobber fishing. And now that she was closer, and Hudson had his hook out of the water, she could see they weren't using floats or sinkers, either. This was the most pathetic fishing effort she'd ever seen.

"What are you trying to catch?"

Hudson shrugged. "Anything."

"Would you mind a few pointers? I mean, you aren't familiar with this lake." She didn't want to point out his complete ignorance in front of his daughter.

"I would be grateful for some pointers."

"Okay. First of all, if you're just going to hang your hook in the water, you need live bait. Minnows, or at least earthworms."

"We don't have any of those things. These fake fish look pretty realistic to me."

Amanda shook her head. "Yes, but you have to wiggle and move them to make them attractive. They won't work if they're just hanging still in the water. Also, most of the fish will already be in deeper water this time of the morning. They come close to shore only at dawn and dusk."

"I don't have any worms or minnows."

"Well…if you're not too particular about what you catch, raw bacon might work in a pinch. At least it smells good to the fish."

Hudson shook his head. "I have hot dogs."

"That might do."

Hudson sent Bethany back to the house for hot dogs, an errand she gladly performed. "She was getting tired of just sitting here, anyway," Hudson admitted.

"Well, she won't be bored when you start catching fish." Bethany dusted off a spot on the dock and sat down, careful to protect her stockings and her modesty in her short skirt. In a couple of minutes flat she had both poles properly outfitted with sinkers, floats and hooks. Bethany returned shortly with a package of franks. Amanda took a small bit of wiener and worked it onto one of the hooks in a way that would disguise it.

"Now. You need to cast your line out a little ways from the dock, and let the current move it along." She and Hudson stood, and she demonstrated the correct procedure. As she stretched her arm back preparing for the cast, she got the distinct impression that Hudson wasn't watching her form—not her fishing form, anyway.

After a few practice casts, Hudson had the technique down pat. He cast Bethany's line for her, showed her how to slowly crank the reel to take up slack in the line, then threw out his own line.

In less than thirty seconds Bethany's bobber wiggled, then plummeted below the surface.

"You've got a fish!" Amanda exclaimed.

Bethany got so excited she shrieked and almost dropped her pole in the water. But with her father standing behind her helping her reel it in, and with Amanda's verbal coaching, she managed to pull a little sunfish out of the water.

"I caught a fish! I caught a fish!"

"Yes, you certainly did," Amanda enthused. "And a magnificent specimen it is, too." It was about three inches long.

"I'm gonna name him Shiny."

Hudson and Amanda exchanged a look. "You didn't tell her what we do with the fish we catch?" Amanda asked.

# Chapter Three

"I figured we'd throw all the fish back," Hudson said.

"No, Daddy, you can't let Shiny go," Bethany said in a near panic. "He's *my* fish."

"Well, he's too small to eat," Amanda said with a laugh.

"Eat!" Bethany's face reflected horror.

Hudson looked to Amanda for some way out of this dilemma. She smiled and shrugged helplessly. "Do you have a bucket to put the fish in?" she asked mildly.

"No." Some help she was! "We're throwing it back in the lake."

"It's *my* fish!" Bethany repeated, her eyes filling with tears.

Amanda's eyes danced with amusement, tempered with concern. "If I were you, I'd let her keep the fish."

Hudson gritted his teeth. He gave Amanda a look that said he wasn't particularly grateful for her suggestion, then turned to his daughter. "Okay, Bethany, here's the deal. You can keep this one fish. But if we catch any more, we have to throw them back. You know, let them swim free, like *Free Willy?*''

''Okay,'' she said without a fight, nodding eagerly.

''And we can't take Shiny back to Boston with us. Fish don't travel well.''

''Unless they're frozen,'' Amanda murmured just loud enough that Hudson could hear.

''Okay,'' Bethany said again.

''Then run up to the house and find a big bowl or a pitcher or a bucket to put the fish in.''

She ran off, leaving Hudson holding the fish.

''Maybe you better dip the line in the water,'' Amanda suggested. ''Shiny's looking a little peaked.''

Hudson did as instructed. The last thing he needed was for Bethany to return and find that her fish had died under his care.

''And I don't want to be an alarmist,'' Amanda added, ''but I think you might have a fish on your line, too.''

Hudson had laid his pole on the dock when he was helping Bethany pull in her fish. He scanned the surface of the lake for the red-and-white bobber and didn't see it anywhere, but his line was taut. He caught the pole just before it would have been pulled into the water.

''Well, don't just stand there, help!''

Amanda took his pole and started reeling in the fish. She could tell by the pull that it was a considerably larger catch than Bethany's. When it finally cleared the water, it turned out to be a huge channel catfish, at least a foot long.

"Wow, beginner's luck," Amanda said, admiring the fish. "Got any pliers?"

"What for?"

"You can't take a catfish off a hook with your bare hands. They sting you with those pointy whiskers."

Hudson had had no idea fishing could be so hazardous. Maybe he should have read a book on the subject first. "I don't have any pliers."

She shook her head as if to say he was hopeless, handed him the pole, then headed up the dock toward her house.

"You're coming back, right?" he asked, feeling slightly panicky himself.

"I've got some pliers in my garage."

Hudson was much relieved by the return of both his daughter and his neighbor. "Shiny" had a new home in a big soup pot, which he set under a tree in the shade for the time being. And Amanda took off her short-sleeved jacket and showed him how to remove a not-too-friendly catfish from a hook.

Hudson and Bethany caught several more fish in all shapes and sizes as Amanda cheered them on and offered pointers. Apparently, Town Lake fish really liked hot dogs—especially Shiny. Bethany kept feeding him bits of wiener.

"That fish is going to get heart disease if we keep feeding him those fatty hot dogs," Hudson grumbled. But he was actually enjoying himself. He liked watching his daughter's eyes light up each time she felt a tug on her line.

And he liked watching Amanda. She'd gotten a snag in her hose and a small spot on her tan linen skirt, but she didn't seem to mind. She appeared to be having fun coaching Hudson and Bethany in the fine art of bobber fishing, as she called it.

"I'm hungry," Bethany announced. "Is it time for lunch yet?"

Hudson looked at his watch. "It's only ten-fifteen."

Amanda jumped like a spooked rabbit. "It's what?" She consulted her own watch. "Oh, my God. Oh, my God! How did it get so late?"

"Late?"

"I've missed my appointment with Clea Marsden." She spied her purse, which she'd set down on the dock, and dived into it, producing a cell phone. "Oh, great, I didn't even have my cell phone on!" She punched in a couple of numbers and waited impatiently for the connection, tapping her foot against the dock.

Bethany watched, fascinated. Hudson confessed to a certain amount of interest himself. His easygoing fishing coach had suddenly turned into a no-nonsense businesswoman.

"Margie? Yes, yes, I'm fine. I just forgot to—no, nothing happened. I lost track of the time. I was…working at home and got involved." Her eyes flickered toward Hudson, perhaps to see if he would call her on the lie, then skittered away. "I must not have heard the phone. I'm sorry I worried you. I hope Clea Marsden wasn't too distressed that I—oh. I see." Her jaw clenched, and a tiny muscle near her eye twitched. "I'll be there in a few minutes." She snapped the phone closed. All the color had drained from her face. In fact, she reminded him of how his mother-in-law had looked when Hudson had told her of her daughter's death.

"Are you all right?" he asked, concerned.

She looked at him as if she was surprised to see him. "No, I'm not all right. I missed an appointment."

"Is that such a tragedy?" he said, trying to lighten the mood.

"Yes! When I didn't show, Clea Marsden got a little antsy, and Mary Jo pounced. I lost the listing." She spoke the words as if it were the worst tragedy to befall Western civilization since the black plague.

"Well, cheer up. Tomorrow's the first day of a new month. You've got all of June to beat Mary Jo."

She seemed not to hear him. "How could I have been so irresponsible, so downright stupid? Fishing, for God's sake! I've frittered away almost three hours! That's time I'll never get back." She looked at him earnestly. "When you waste time, you never get it back, you know."

He did know that—all too well. Often he felt there weren't enough hours in the day to accomplish all he wanted to do. There were always more patients than he had time to operate on. Once, a patient at the hospital—not his, thank God—had died while waiting for a free operating room.

"I'm very aware of how I spend my time," he said, his good mood deflated. He shouldn't be here. He should be back in Boston, doing what he was meant to do.

Amanda pulled a towelette from her purse and began rubbing at the small spot on her skirt. "I've torn my stockings, I've stained my skirt, I probably have a sunburn and I know I smell like fish. What on earth was I thinking? I must be out of my mind.''

"Hey, easy on the self-flagellation. Everybody loses track of the time now and then.''

"Not me. Not when I've got bills to pay and people depending on me. I have to think of my future. No one's going to take care of me when I'm old.''

Good heavens, she was serious.

"I have to go. Thank you again for fixing the bad check. Good luck with your fishing.'' She turned and started away.

"Amanda?'' Bethany called after her. "Wait.''

Amanda turned back, looking flushed and slightly guilty. "Yes, Bethany, what is it?''

"Could you help me make a place for Shiny to live?''

"Well, I think your dad can probably help you.''

"But he doesn't even like Shiny.''

"I'm really busy, sweetheart. I…'' Amanda looked to Hudson for support, but he refused to give her any. She was the one, after all, who'd insisted Bethany ought to keep the damn fish as a pet. "Well, all right. But later, when I'm done with work, okay?''

"Okay.''

Hudson watched as she picked her way across the uneven ground in her high heels.

"Where does Amanda work?'' Bethany asked.

"At the real estate office, remember? She helps people buy and sell and rent houses.''

"Does she get paid money?''

"Yes. For every house she sells or rents, she gets a certain percentage of the price.''

Bethany stared at him quizzically. Okay, so commissions were probably a little much for a four-year-old to comprehend.

"Say a house is a pie," he tried again. "It's my pie and I want to sell it. Amanda knows someone who wants to buy a pie, so she introduces the two of us. I sell the pie to this other person—but I give Amanda one slice as her reward for finding the buyer."

Bethany wrinkled her nose. "So this person buys a pie with a piece gone?"

"Never mind. I'm tired of fishing, how about you?"

She nodded.

Was ten-thirty too early for lunch? Nah. They were still on Boston time, he reminded himself, and they'd had those Pop-Tarts before the sun was up. They gathered up the fishing gear and returned it to the garage. Then Hudson carried Bethany's fish to the house. The pot seemed awfully small. He really, really didn't want the fish to die. So he put the stopper in the bathtub, filled it up and transferred Shiny to another new home.

"I guess Shiny needs an aquarium," Hudson said as he studied the fish swimming around.

Bethany knew what an aquarium was. Apparently they had a big one at her preschool. She talked endlessly about it and drew pictures of the fish. Hell, maybe he had a budding marine biologist on his hands, and he should encourage her interest in fish. But she didn't respond to his suggestion with the enthusiasm he'd hoped.

"Amanda's going to help me make a house for Shiny."

Hudson hoped Bethany didn't put too much stock

in Amanda's promises. She seemed to be a nice person, and she'd certainly established a rapport with his daughter. But she was obviously far too devoted to her job to want to cater to the whims of a four-year-old neighbor.

Before seeing about lunch, Hudson went into his bedroom and dug out his blood-pressure cuff. He'd been fishing all morning. Surely all that relaxation would have knocked his blood pressure down a few points. He slid his arm into the cuff and pumped it up, feeling optimistic.

"One-fifty-two over one-ten!" That was ridiculous. His blood pressure was higher than it had been in the doctor's office. It was just a fluke, he told himself. He would take it again when he wasn't thinking about Amanda.

HUDSON TOOK HIS blood pressure four times that afternoon. The numbers simply wouldn't go down. He had to face it, he had high blood pressure. Continued hypertension could lead to all sorts of unpleasant things, including making him a candidate for his own brand of medicine. Well, he wasn't going to turn into one of those people—overweight, unable to walk a flight of stairs without huffing and puffing. He would get his blood pressure down.

He still had all of June to do it. Although he was going to go crazy if he had to stay in this cabin for a month. There was nothing to do!

A shopping trip was in order, he decided. He would buy some books, some games he and Bethany could play, maybe some crafts. He could take up gardening. That was supposed to be relaxing.

What other advice did he give his heart patients? Meditation. Yoga. He doubted he would find any type of class around here, but maybe he could find a book instructing him on the practices. Healthy meals.

He opened the freezer and pondered the contents. Frozen pizza. Battered fish sticks—better not go there. Bethany still didn't quite get the concept that much of the food they ate used to be walking around or flying or swimming. TV dinners—all of them loaded with fat grams. Even the lunch meat he'd bought was the bad kind—ham, pepperoni, beefstick. Combine them with cheese and mayonnaise, and you had a heart attack sandwich.

A movement outside caught his eye. A car pulled into Amanda's driveway, but not Amanda's silver Lincoln. It was a red compact car, a few years old, with numerous dents and scrapes and one badly crumpled fender. A young man got out—a kid, really. The resemblance between him and Amanda was hard to miss—same white-blond hair, same cheekbones. He wore holey jeans and a tank shirt revealing lots of muscles and a prominent tattoo.

The young man walked around the car and opened the passenger door. A statuesque brunette in miniskirt and halter top unfolded herself and climbed out. The way the two touched each other, it was clear they were lovers. The man let himself in the front door with a key, and the couple disappeared inside.

"Is Amanda home from work?" Bethany asked excitedly, apparently seeing her father staring out the window.

"Haven't seen her yet. You know, honey, Amanda seems pretty busy. I wouldn't count on her to just drop everything and help you with a home for your fish."

"Yes, she will help me," Bethany said with the utter faith only a child could muster.

"Couldn't I help you?"

"No. You don't like Shiny. You wanted to eat him."

"I wanted to throw him back." Amanda was the one who'd wanted to eat the fish, but Hudson decided not to point that out. "You know, honey, people do eat fish. When you eat fish sticks? Those are fish that used to swim in the ocean."

Bethany adopted a mutinous expression. "Nuh-uh. Fish sticks are square and they don't have eyes."

"An important distinction," Hudson agreed, giving up. "Hey, I've got an idea. Why don't we go out to dinner?"

"To McDonald's?" she asked hopefully.

Bethany was addicted to Happy Meals. He really ought to nudge her in a different dietary direction. "Cottonwood doesn't have a McDonald's. I thought we could be adventurous. You know, try someplace new."

"No. I want to stay here and wait for Amanda."

Hudson was afraid it would be a very long wait.

He made bologna sandwiches for dinner, and they ate them at a picnic table on a small deck in back. Once it had been cleaned, this little cabin really wasn't so bad, he decided. From here he had a nice view of the woods…and an unobstructed view of Amanda's house. He saw when her brother—if that's who it was—left again with the brunette, who looked quite a bit more disheveled than when she'd arrived. He could guess what they'd been up to.

Bethany watched Amanda's house, too, and the yearning on her face was plain. She was accustomed to female companionship—one or the other of her grandmothers had been in constant attendance since Elaine's death. Being around her father all the time was a big adjustment. But Hudson was determined that she get used to him—and vice versa.

She resisted going to bed, still wanting to wait for Amanda. "She probably had to work late," Hudson said, trying to soothe her. "Sometimes grown-ups have to work long hours. She might need the extra money."

"But you work *all* the time, and you're rich."

Another prickle of guilt. "People work long hours for other reasons besides money. In my case, I work because my patients need me. They need someone to fix their hearts."

"But maybe *my* heart needs fixing."

"I hope not. Not ever."

"But it hurts sometimes."

The backs of Hudson's eyes burned. "Everyone's heart hurts sometimes. When you feel like yours is hurting, you just call me and I'll do my best to fix it."

"It hurts now."

"Why does it hurt, sweetie?"

"Because Shiny doesn't have a good house." And because Amanda had disappointed her. He might not be too experienced with this daddy business, but he could read between the lines.

He took her hand and led her toward the ladder that went to the loft. ''Tomorrow we're gonna build Shiny the best aquarium in all of Texas.''

''Will Amanda help?''

Hudson tamped down his frustration. Bethany barely knew Amanda. Why this sudden attachment? ''We'll ask her. But if she can't, then just you and me, okay?''

''Okay,'' she said grudgingly.

With a bit more coaxing, he got her into bed. Then he sat on the back deck, smoking his last cigarette and watching for Amanda. It really was his last cigarette, he promised himself. Although he wasn't exactly a heavy smoker—he'd taken a week to get through this last pack—the blood-pressure thing was scaring him. Smoking was one thing he could control.

Since he had time to kill, and he was already in a bad mood, he checked the messages on his cell. It was pretty much as he'd feared.

''Hudson, this is your mother. Call me immediately. I need some investment advice....''

''Hudson, it's Janey. I need to know for sure whether you're going to the fund-raiser Friday. Call me.''

''Hudson, it's your mother. Just what in heaven's name does that message on your voice mail mean? Unavailable? How do you expect people to get in touch with you?''

''Hudson, it's Janey. I'm getting a little miffed over

your lack of communication. I have to make some decisions, and I can't without your input. Honestly..."

"Hudson, this is your mother. If you don't call me in the next thirty minutes, I'm calling the police. I'm afraid some chainsaw serial killer has found you."

Reluctantly he called his mother. He nearly jumped for joy when he reached her answering machine. "Mother, it's Hudson. I'm fine, Bethany's fine. Our vacation is going well. I'll speak with you when I get back." He disconnected as quickly as he could, in case she was home and screening her calls.

Janey wouldn't be so easy. He called her cell, hoping to get her voice mail. But she answered immediately, though it was after eleven Boston time. "Hudson, thank God. Where are you?"

"I'm on vacation with Bethany. Didn't I tell you...?"

"You know perfectly well you didn't tell me. If you'd let me know, I could have cleared my schedule and gone with you. Are you at your mother's place in Martha's Vineyard? I could join you there in a couple of days."

"No!" That was all he needed. He would never relax with Janey around managing his social schedule. "I mean, um, I'm doing a little father-daughter bonding."

"Oh, that's so sweet! Where are you?"

"Someplace you've never heard of, I guarantee."

"When will you be back?"

"I don't really know. I'll call back when my plans are firmed up."

"Hudson, this is so unlike you. You never do anything impulsive. Now, I want you to tell me where you are.''

He didn't care for her demanding tone. If he married her, he'd probably hear more of it, he realized. ''I have to go, um, the stove's boiling over.''

''The stove? You've never been near a stove in your life!''

''I'll talk to you later,'' he said with mock cheerfulness. ''Bye!'' He hung up on her sputtered objections, then quickly turned off his phone.

Amanda's car finally pulled into the drive at ten forty-five. No one worked that late, not even Hudson. It occurred to him that she might have a social life. She might have been enjoying dinner with a date, or happy hour with some girlfriends. But if she'd made plans for after work, she should have told Bethany upfront that she couldn't help with Shiny's home today. And if the plans had been spur-of-the-moment, then she'd needlessly broken her word to his daughter.

And he wasn't going to let that pass without comment.

WHEN AMANDA SAW the mess her house was in, her blood flashed through her veins like heat lightning. For heaven's sake, couldn't Mick make even the smallest effort to clean up after himself? Dirty dishes from what looked like breakfast *and* lunch littered the kitchen. The mail had been strewn about the living room, items of interest opened and left where they fell. Cushions had been pulled off the couch in front of the TV. Dirty clothes carpeted the bathroom floor.

How had she let herself become Mick's maid?

When her father had died three years ago, she'd naturally been sad, but she'd also been relieved to be free of the burden of taking care of him. Especially the last few years, he hadn't been able to drive or cook or do his own laundry, so she'd done those things for him, recycling the empty beer cans without comment. She'd known that by then it was too late to change him. Back then, Mick had lived with their father, and while he hadn't exactly helped, he'd been in high school, so she'd let him get away with a lot.

Then they'd sold her dad's house, which the bank was about to foreclose on anyway, and Mick had moved in with her so he could go to college. But in all this time he'd made little progress toward a degree, and he'd become increasingly irresponsible and decadent. She feared his drinking was to blame, though he at least had the consideration not to drink in front of her.

She wished she had the courage to just leave his messes. How would he like it if the house just turned into a pigsty?

Shoot, he probably wouldn't even notice until he ran out of clean clothes.

She started to run a load of Mick's laundry, then stopped when she smelled the beer and cigarettes that permeated the clothes. How could he sit around in bars having a good time, then drop half his class load every semester and still claim he didn't have time for a job? And where was he now, anyway? He would claim he was studying.

In a fit of anger, she gathered up the clothes and carried them to Mick's room, where she heaved them onto the bed. Mick could wash his own damn clothes. And he could clean up his own dishes. She gathered up the plates and silverware and sticky, half-empty glasses and stacked them on Mick's dresser. She tossed his discarded mail in there, too. Then she cleaned drips off the counters and sticky footprints from the floors until the place was in its preferred spotless condition.

She would *not* let her house go to rack and ruin. She'd worked too hard for it.

The doorbell rang just as Amanda was putting away the mop. Had Mick forgotten his key again? Or was it the cops, come to tell her Mick had been in a terrible accident?

*Stop that!* Why did her mind always conjure up a worst-case scenario for every situation?

She opened the door. In a million years, she never would have guessed that Hudson Stack would be standing on her porch at almost eleven o'clock in the evening, scowling.

# Chapter Four

"Oh, hi," Amanda said uncertainly. She opened the door to allow Hudson inside, glad she'd cleaned. It wasn't often she had guests.

He stepped in, but he didn't stop staring at her. He certainly wasn't noticing whether any dust bunnies were lurking.

"You're home awfully late," he said.

"I had a lot of work to catch up on."

"So you were at the office all this time?"

"Well, at the office, and showing houses—a lot of people want to look at houses after work." What was this? She wondered. Why did he care what hours she worked? Then she remembered. Bethany. She'd carelessly told the little girl she would help her fix up someplace for Shiny the Fish to live.

Her hand flew to her mouth. "I'm sorry," she said immediately. "I'm so sorry. I forgot all about your daughter. How's the fish?" She led him into the living room and indicated he should sit down, but he remained standing.

"Alive and well, and living in our bathtub, thanks to you."

Amanda couldn't help the small laugh that escaped. "Oh, come on. You would have lost that battle whether I was there or not."

"It's your fault she caught the damn fish in the first place."

"And I suppose you would have preferred fishing like a complete incompetent, never even getting a nibble?"

"Yes. Then we would have given up and found something else to do. Now Bethany's addicted. She wants to do it again tomorrow."

"And what's wrong with that? Fishing is a wonderful way to bond with your kids," Amanda said. "My own father and I used to fish for hours, all summer long. And we cleaned and ate the fish, too." Sometimes those fish were all that stood in the way of going to bed hungry.

"Well maybe *he'd* like to take Bethany fishing."

"I'm afraid that would be a bit difficult. He's dead."

Hudson raked his fingers through his short hair. "Sorry about that. I didn't think before I spoke."

"It's okay. What are you really mad at me for?"

Now he did sit down. He looked weary down to the cellular level. "For disappointing Bethany, that's all. I know you didn't exactly make a hard-and-fast promise, but you have to be careful what you say to kids her age. They take things very literally. You said 'after work,' which for you could mean today or tomorrow or next weekend. But to a four-year-old, that meant she expected you to show up at our house at five o'clock with an aquarium and gravel and plastic plants.''

"I'm sorry, really. I confess, I don't have much experience with children."

"Well, you must be doing something right. She sure liked you. Every other word out of her mouth today was 'Amanda this' and 'Amanda that.'''

Amanda was surprised at the flush of pleasure she felt. She'd never had a child get attached to her before, not since Mick had been little. She'd been six when he was born, and she'd taken great pleasure in helping her mother care for him, even declaring that he was *her* baby. His attachment to her had lasted just until he'd figured out he was a boy and she was a girl and he was supposed to hate girls.

Hudson must have caught her smiling. "This isn't funny. She was really upset that you never showed up."

"I wasn't smiling about that. I was just thinking of something else. So how can I make this right? Should I go over right now and apologize?"

"Bethany's asleep."

"Of course. At this hour, she would be. I'll do it tomorrow, how about that? We used to have an aquarium at the office. I think it's in the storage room. I can bring that home. We can clean it up and at least get started."

Hudson didn't show much enthusiasm for her idea. He was still frowning.

"What?"

"I just don't want you to make promises you can't keep, that's all."

"Of course I'll keep my word. Except…" Oh, hell. She ran to where she'd dropped her briefcase and dug into it for her palmtop. A couple of buttons later and she had her schedule in front of her. Tomorrow she had a meeting at six and another at eight. Actually, her schedule was completely packed tomorrow. But maybe after lunch, if she rescheduled the Desmond showing to an hour later…

"You don't have time, do you?" Hudson said, almost triumphantly.

"I do. I just have to work things out."

"How many hours do you work in a day?"

She shrugged. "I've never stopped to count. I guess about ten on a normal day." Or twelve. Or fourteen. If she were honest, she would admit that most days she didn't get home before eight o'clock, and often it was later.

"And is that your normal dinner?" he said, nodding to the can of Slimfast.

"It's quick, easy, low in fat and nutritionally balanced. What else could you ask for?"

"How about fiber? Omega-3 fatty acids?"

"You sound like my doctor."

He flashed a startled look before quickly recovering. "I've read quite a bit about nutrition, that's all. Have you checked your blood pressure lately?"

"Why would I have a blood pressure problem? I'm not overweight and I don't smoke."

"What about exercise?"

"What is this, a wellness interrogation? Have you suddenly turned into the health police?" She laughed as she said it, but she felt defensive. What business of his was her lifestyle?

"Just concerned, that's all."

"Well, save it for someone who needs it."

Her brother chose that moment to arrive home. He came in through the garage door, and he wasn't alone. She groaned inwardly. This place was becoming a regular Grand Central Station, when all she wanted was to have her bath and go to bed.

"Hey, sis. You remember Tonya, right?"

Amanda pasted on a smile. Oh, yeah, she remembered Tonya Green. Big hair, big boobs, not too bright, worked at the Dairy Queen. "Hi, Tonya, nice to see you again." She introduced them to Hudson, who'd been edging toward the door after her rebuke. They all murmured a greeting. Mick looked right through Hudson, the way he did with anyone over the age of thirty, dismissing him as nonimportant. Tonya, however, gave him a quick head-to-toe and a sultry smile that said his finer qualities weren't lost on her.

"C'mon." Mick took Tonya's hand and tugged her toward his room. Tonya followed reluctantly. That was when Amanda remembered what she'd done in her fit of pique.

"Um, Mick? Can I talk to you a minute?"

"Later."

Amanda cringed as Mick opened the door, and the inevitable explosion followed.

"What the hell did you do in here? What is all this crap?"

Amanda girded her loins and prepared to do battle. But first she had to deal with Hudson. She certainly didn't want him to be a witness to the nasty argument that was surely coming. She saw him to the door. "I'll be by around one tomorrow to apologize to Bethany, if that's okay."

Hudson looked uncertain. "If I tell her you're coming, and you don't show up—"

"I'll be there." Just as she was more or less shoving him out the door, she got the undeniable whiff of cigarettes. "Mick? Have you been smoking?" she yelled over her shoulder.

"Um, that's probably me."

"You? You smoke? Oh, you're a fine one to lecture about a healthy diet."

"I quit."

"When?"

"About half an hour ago. I'm not smoking anymore, really."

"It's nothing to me if you want to kill yourself, but you really should think about Bethany." With that she managed to close the door between them.

HUDSON RETURNED TO his cabin, checked on Bethany, then went back outside. He wished he *had* another cigarette. Just one, to work off the nervous energy. And he had plenty of that after spending a few minutes in Amanda's house, watching her dart about in hyperdrive. She hadn't been like that when they were fishing. In fact, this morning her movements had been smooth, languorous. She'd talked slower, smiled a lot.

Hudson had a sneaking suspicion that Amanda Dew-hurst needed to slow down and smell the roses even more than he did. She had stress written all over her, and he'd seen it in enough people to recognize it. Sure, she was young. But if she didn't mend her ways, she would pay for her careless lifestyle later. It was hard to undo years of damage to your organs and blood vessels.

She didn't seem the type to be converted, though. She was a workaholic, pure and simple. He understood exactly where she was coming from, since he was a member of that club, too. But he, at least, was starting to see the light. His elevated blood pressure had been a wake-up call.

Amanda did seem to have a soft spot for Bethany, though. Maybe through his daughter, he could convince Amanda to at least moderate her lifestyle, if not give it a radical overhaul. This month spent in the hinterlands would certainly be easier to swallow if he had someone interesting to spend it with. And Amanda was very interesting.

AMANDA WAS DETERMINED to keep her word to Hudson. She would be at the cabin at one o'clock, and she would bring the old aquarium with her. She spent her lunch digging it out of the storage room, along with some gravel and plastic plants.

"What on earth are you doing?" Margie asked when she returned from her own lunch and stuck her head through the storeroom door.

"It's a long story."

"I've got time." Margie squeezed into the storeroom and plopped down on a broken chair.

"I promised a little girl I would help her set up an aquarium. No one cares if I take this, do they?" Margie's husband, Jerry, the broker who owned Tri-County Real Estate, pretty much gave Margie and his agents carte blanche to do whatever they wanted with the office, so long as they continued to sell houses.

"Oh, sure, take it," Margie said. "We should clear more junk out of here, anyway. Wait a minute. You're bonding with some little girl?" Margie laughed.

"I'm not bonding," Amanda said quickly. "I don't do kids. You know that. She sort of tricked me into it."

"Does this have something to do with your being late yesterday?"

"If you must know, yes. It's my new neighbors. I feel sorry for them."

"Why?"

"Because they seem kind of lost. I get the feeling they don't really want to be on this vacation. Either Hudson got fired and he's at loose ends, or he has visitation with his daughter for the first time in forever and he doesn't know what to do with her, or both."

"So you've found someone else who needs you to take care of them. Great."

Amanda sent Margie a sharp look. "What's that supposed to mean?"

"Just that if you took care of yourself the way you take care of everybody else, you'd be a whole lot happier."

"I *am* happy! And what am I supposed to do, kick Mick out in the street? He's in school."

"He's out every night at the Red Dog Saloon while you're slaving away here."

Amanda stilled. "He is?"

"That's what I hear."

Amanda sank on to a box. "He's entitled to relax sometimes."

"Amanda, honey, if that boy got any more relaxed you'd have to stake him up just so he could watch TV."

"I guess it's time I had a talk with him."

"Has that ever worked before?"

She thought about the argument they'd had last night. She'd blustered. He'd retaliated. She'd stood firm. He'd collapsed and given her that scolded-puppy look, and promised to try harder. And in the end, she'd washed his damn dishes.

"No."

"Actions speak louder than words. Kick him out."

"What?"

"Mick isn't going to take responsibility for his own life so long as he's getting a free ride. Kick him out. Force him to grow up. You'll be doing him a favor."

"I can't do that! I promised Dad I'd look after Mick."

"Not into infinity."

"Hello," a voice called out. "Is anyone here?"

"Oops." Margie hopped off her chair and headed for the front office. "Sorry, ma'am, didn't hear you come in. Can I help you?"

Carrying the aquarium and whatever peripherals she'd been able to find, Amanda followed Margie out, curious about the newcomer. Standing in front of Margie's desk was a tall, attractive couple with expectant looks on their faces.

"We're interested in buying a vacation house in this area, maybe on the lake," the man said.

"I can help you," Amanda said, setting the aquarium down and wiping the grime off her hands with a tissue. "I'm Amanda Dewhurst." She shook hands with the couple.

Margie cleared her throat. Noisily. Twice. When Amanda looked at her, annoyed, Margie discreetly pointed to her watch.

Amanda consulted her own watch. It was ten minutes to one. Shoot. Shoot, shoot, shoot! "Oh, gosh, Margie has just reminded me I have an appointment. I'd be happy to talk to you at four o'clock."

"We have to head home before then," the woman said apologetically.

She could call Hudson, she thought. She could reschedule her time with—no. She wasn't going to do that. She would be major pond scum if she broke her promise again.

It was like choking on sawdust to get the words out, but Amanda managed it. "I'm sure one of the other agents can help you. Margie? Is Emily in?"

HUDSON WAS ACTUALLY SURPRISED when he spotted Amanda's car coming up his driveway. Bethany, who'd been watching out the window like a cat waiting for a mouse to come out of hiding, jumped up and ran for the door. "She's here, Amanda's here!"

"Take it easy, Beth. You'll scare the poor woman away."

But Bethany wasn't listening. She barreled out the

door and nearly knocked Amanda over with her enthusiastic hug.

The attachment still baffled him. He couldn't remember seeing Bethany hug anyone like that, especially not him. She sometimes took his hand, and she tolerated it when he kissed her good-night, but she'd never just thrown her arms around him spontaneously.

That was horrible, he realized. He hadn't just been a careless father, or unthinking, or working too hard. He'd been neglectful. Of course, spontaneous shows of affection weren't exactly a hallmark of the Stack family. He couldn't remember his father ever hugging him. And his mother, though he was reasonably sure she loved him, restricted herself to air kisses somewhere in the vicinity of his cheek.

That was one legacy he didn't intend to pass on. He'd have to do better.

Amanda and Bethany were rooting around in Amanda's trunk by the time Hudson reached them at his more sedate pace. Amanda was dressed casually today, he noticed, in a ribbed, ice-blue T-shirt, knee-length khaki skirt, bare legs and sparkly sandals. Her hair was still scraped back in that no-nonsense do, though. How much would he have to pay her to get her to take it down? Let him run his fingers through it?

He could think of a lot of places he'd like to run his fingers. But he supposed that was out of the question. He didn't even know if she had a boyfriend lurking somewhere. If she did, he was probably lonely.

"This aquarium was sitting around at the office," she explained as they headed for the cabin, each of them carrying something. "We'll have to scrub it down, and I'm not sure this pump works."

"We have to have a pump," Bethany said, sounding slightly alarmed. "Fish get air out of the water, and the pump makes bubbles so the fish can breathe."

"That's right. How did you learn that?"

"We have fish at my school."

Hudson made a mental note to send that school a big check. Apparently they were teaching his daughter something, at least.

"Well, if we can't get the pump to work, we'll run up to the pet store and buy a new one. How about that?"

"Okay."

Amanda and Bethany talked and giggled as they scrubbed the aquarium in the cabin's ancient kitchen sink. Hudson mainly tried to stay out of the way. There was female bonding going on, and he wanted no part of it. Except that he stayed close enough so he could listen to them. The sound of Bethany's laughter was like a balm to his soul.

On a whim, he checked his blood pressure again. Ah-ha, just as he'd surmised. His systolic was down by four points, the diastolic by two. At this rate, he could be back home in a week or two.

He sat in the cabin's main room on an uncomfortable couch and read a book he'd found on bass fishing. Man, he'd had no idea it was so complicated. He was adding words to his vocabulary by the minute— lunker, spoon plug, whisker bug, skittering. He studied diagrams of complicated knots that, if mastered, could add some panache to his surgery techniques. The in-

tricacies of bass fishing made heart surgery look like
a walk in the park. Apparently, fish were smart. You
had to outthink them. He'd never had to outthink a
heart.

A few minutes later a shadow fell across his book.
Amanda and Bethany stood before him, looking som-
ber.

"Here's the deal," Amanda said. "We can't get the
pump to work, so we have to go buy a new one. Is
that okay?"

"Sure." He closed the book and stood. "It'll be
good to get out of the house."

"Oh, you're coming with us?"

"You don't want me to?"

"No, we want you to come," Bethany piped in.

They rode in Amanda's car to the town square.
Hudson really hadn't paid much attention when they'd
come here before, but now he did. With the ancient
live oaks in the center of the square and the quaint
architecture and colorful awnings of all the shops surrounding it, downtown Cottonwood was a trip back in
time. He'd seen nothing else in Texas quite like it.

In fact, this whole part of Texas had surprised him.
He'd been expecting desert and cactus. But here in the
eastern part of the state it was all rolling hills, pine
trees and lush farmland.

And lots of cows. He'd promised Bethany that
sometime during this trip, he would allow her to pet
a cow. Ed Hardison had said something about one of
his sons working the family ranch.

Bethany went nuts at the pet store. There wasn't a
guinea pig or parakeet in the whole place she didn't

want to take home with her. Hudson was beginning to wonder if coming to town with the ladies was such a great idea. But Amanda got her settled down once they started shopping for fish paraphernalia.

Hudson again stayed out of the way, petting a guinea pig. The thing was remarkably cute. He'd never had a pet. His mother had always claimed she was allergic.

When it came time to pay the bill, Hudson reached for his wallet, but Amanda was faster. "No, let me get this," she said. "Since this whole fish thing is mostly my fault…"

It was only a few dollars, and it was such a novel experience, having a woman pay for something, that he let her do it. Then it occurred to him that Amanda thought he was poor. Bethany had told her he was out of work; he'd rented the nastiest cabin on the lake; and his check had bounced.

He decided he wouldn't disabuse her of the notion. Let her think she was doing something charitable, donating her time and her aquarium to the poor single dad and his deprived child. At least he would know she liked him—if she *did* like him—for himself and not his money or status as a big-time surgeon. It hurt to realize it, but he didn't think Janey would give him the time of day if he wasn't a Stack.

Amanda and Bethany joined him at the door. "Here's the deal," Amanda said. "They had the pump, but they're out of spun glass for the filter. The lady says we can use fake cotton balls from the drugstore. So would you mind if we made an extra stop? It's on the way home."

"Please, Daddy?"

"Sure. Why not?"

There was a drugstore on the highway out toward the lake. Hudson needed to buy some batteries for his Walkman, so he could listen to baseball games or talk radio or something. The lack of TV was getting to him.

In the corner of the store, he spotted one of those take-your-own-blood-pressure machines, and it gave him an idea. He bought his batteries, then waited for Amanda and Bethany to purchase whatever they needed. Then he set his trap.

"So, Amanda. Care to lay a little wager with me?"

She gave him a blank look. "What on earth are you talking about?"

"You claim there's no way you could have high blood pressure. I'm betting you're wrong."

She groaned. "I thought you'd let this go."

"There's a machine in the corner where you can measure. If it's normal, I'll take you out to dinner."

She batted her eyes at him. "If you wanted to take me to dinner, why didn't you just ask?"

"And if it's high, you have to do something for me."

She narrowed her eyes. "Like what?"

"Teach Bethany and me how to fish."

"What? You've gotta be kidding. I thought you didn't like fishing."

"I might like it, if I knew how, and if I had the right equipment. Ed Hardison said I can borrow his boat anytime I want."

"I don't have time for fishing lessons."

"Exactly my point."

"What point?"

"You're driven. Driven people end up on my—"
He stopped. He'd almost said, *end up on my operating
table.* But he still wasn't willing to reveal to anyone
his true vocation. The anonymity was so very, very
nice.

"End up where?"

"End up having heart attacks. Or getting congestive
heart failure."

"Why do you care about all this?"

How to answer that and not lie? He wanted to tell
her that his most fervent wish was to reduce the number of patients who needed his skills. Then he
wouldn't have to work so hard. Instead he said, "My
father died of a heart attack."

"I'm sorry. Was it recent?"

"No, not at all. I was still in college. But he was
young, thin, didn't smoke. But he worked *all the time.*
Just like you." Just like he did.

"So you assume I'm headed for the same fate.
That's silly. Millions of people work hard and don't
have heart attacks."

"Millions do. I won't bore you with the statistics.
There's an easier way to convince you." He nodded
toward the machine. "Do we have a bet?"

She shrugged. "Sure. If some silly test will lay your
fears to rest, I'll be happy to take it." She set down
her things and sat on the bench, sliding her arm
through the cuff. Her finger wavered over the start
button. "Don't watch me. It makes me nervous."

"Okay." Not that he didn't like watching her. She

was pretty easy on the eyes. She was pretty, period. But when he stared at her...well, suffice it to say, it wasn't good for his own blood pressure.

He took a couple of steps back and studied a display of antacids. Funny, but he hadn't needed any since leaving Boston. He heard the machine start up. A few seconds later he heard an indignant screech.

"One-fifty-five over one-eleven!"

Hudson studied the digital readout himself. Good heavens, she was in the red zone. Hers was worse than his. His momentary surge of pleasure at being right was eclipsed for his concern, now more than just passing, over her health.

"This machine is broken. It has to be." She surrendered her seat. "Here, you try it."

"That won't prove much. Mine's high, too. Why don't we go to Dr. Hardison's office?"

"I don't have time for that. Let's just go finish the aquarium."

"What about our bet?"

"We didn't shake on it."

"You're going to renege based on a technicality?"

She had the grace to look guilty. "I couldn't possibly—" She stopped.

"Your promises don't hold a lot of weight, do they?"

She flushed, but whether from embarrassment or anger he couldn't tell. "Fishing lessons?"

"Every day."

"I'll give you two hours, three times a week."

He was amazed she'd given in. "Done. Starting tomorrow?"

She hesitated, then nodded.

"And just to show you I'm a gracious winner, I'll take you out to dinner, anyway."

"Impossible. I'll be too busy catching up on all the work I'll be giving up while I'm teaching you to fish." With that she picked up her things and headed out the door, chin high, hips swaying beneath her khaki skirt. He and Bethany hurried to catch up, for fear she'd drive away without them.

# Chapter Five

As Amanda drove to the Cottonwood Marina, she found herself fuming again. How had Hudson Stack manipulated her so thoroughly? Fishing lessons! How in the world was she going to find six extra hours in her week?

But he'd gotten to her with that comment about the worth of her promises. Of course she kept her promises. She'd shown up with the fish tank for Shiny, hadn't she? And she'd kept the two biggest promises of her life, both made at the bedside of a dying parent.

Her mother had begged her to take care of her father. *He means well. He's just weak. You and I, we're strong. It's up to us to take care of the weak ones.*

She'd promised, and she'd taken care of him. She'd dragged him to treatment centers and AA meetings. She'd propped him up in the shower when he was too hung over to stand. She'd found jobs for him—which he always managed to lose after a few weeks. She'd made sure his bills were paid. And finally, she'd sat by his bedside as he lay dying and made yet another promise, this time to take care of Mick.

Was history repeating itself? Was she ultimately harming Mick by sheltering him from the repercussions of his own irresponsibility?

Well, here she was, worrying about things again. And Hudson had given her something else to worry about—her blood pressure. Who could have guessed it was so high? But it was. She'd had Ed Hardison's nurse, Sherry, double-check it at Ed's office. It was high, way high, and she'd earned herself a lecture from Dr. Ed himself about slowing down and destressing and worrying less. He'd handed her a booklet on controlling blood pressure, which she'd practically memorized.

All right, so maybe fishing would be good for her, even if it did put her work schedule in a bind.

Hudson and Bethany were waiting for her on the dock, and some of her irritation fled. Bethany looked so cute in a little polka-dot shorts outfit with a matching hat, her dark curls peeking out around the edges. And Hudson? He was a little beyond cute in cutoff shorts and a T-shirt that revealed way more of his muscular arms and legs and broad chest than made her comfortable. He wore a hat, too, a battered thing that looked like the one Gilligan wore. She'd told them to wear hats and sunscreen because the Texas sun out on the water was more than fierce.

Amanda wore her own hat, a baseball cap with the Tri-County Realty logo on it. Otherwise, she was overdressed for fishing, in a white cotton blouse and khaki slacks, but she didn't have time to change.

Bethany spotted her and ran to her, throwing her

chubby arms around Amanda's hips. "Yea! You're here! We're gonna ride on a boat!"

"Have you never been on a boat before?"

"No, but I rode a merry-go-round once."

Hudson greeted her with a big smile. "You made it." That smile caused a little hitch in Amanda's heart, which she ruthlessly ignored. She did not live to make Hudson Stack smile, she reminded herself.

"I told you I would. Am I going to spend the rest of my life making up that one eensy-beensy broken promise? Because I'm usually pretty trustworthy."

"Maybe not the rest of your life," he said. "A year or two, though."

"Very funny."

"Did you stop by Ed Hardison's office and get the key?"

She pulled the key, attached to a foam-rubber float, from her purse. "And while I was there, I had him check my blood pressure."

"And?"

She sighed. "Dismal. I guess it's something I have to work on."

"Don't look so glum about it. I have to get mine lower, too. We can work on it together."

She brightened. "Could we make it like a contest? Whoever lowers their blood pressure the most gets, um…" *Gets to kiss the other one senseless.* Oh, my, she really did need to get control of her wayward thoughts.

"Competition really spurs you on, huh?"

"Yes. A simple goal isn't good enough. I have to

have someone to beat.'' She grinned. It wasn't so hard, admitting her faults.

''I think we should make this a group project,'' he said diplomatically. ''We'll help each other.''

''That's not nearly as much fun.'' But he was probably right. Competition would be counterproductive.

Bethany sighed impatiently. ''Would you two stop talking so we can go on the boat?''

''All right.'' Amanda ruffled Bethany's dark curls. ''It's this way, slip number seven.''

Berthed in slip seven was a huge bass boat with room for at least eight passengers. It was a far cry from the little dinghies Amanda and her father used to beg, borrow and on occasion borrow without permission to get their fishing fix, but Amanda had spent enough time around boats to know her bow from her stern. She didn't think she would have any trouble handling it.

After equipping herself and her passengers with life jackets, she untied all the lines, pulled in the bumpers, and started up the engine. She backed the boat slowly out of its slip, and a familiar anticipation stole over her.

She loved boating. She loved the smell of the water, the wind in her hair, the feel of the sun on her skin. She loved the sound of the waves lapping against the boat's hull, and watching the lazy water birds that wheeled overhead.

How long had it been since she'd been in a boat? Probably the Chatsworths' fish fry last year, when Milton Chatsworth had taken a group out on his pontoon boat for an evening cruise. And then the two older

Hardison brothers had gotten into a fist fight over little Allison Crane, who was now married to one of them, she forgot which.

Maybe when Mick graduated, she would celebrate by buying herself a little boat. Someday, maybe, when every penny didn't go into making ends meet.

"Where are we going?" Bethany asked, breaking into Amanda's reverie.

"Somewhere the fish might be biting. In the heat of the afternoon, the bass will be hanging out deep, out of the sun. What we need is a little cove with some shade and some sunken logs."

"How about over there?" Hudson pointed to an attractive, deserted inlet with a narrow strip of sandy beach.

"No, the wind is heading the wrong way." She explained to him about how a light breeze blowing into the cove was best, and she realized she had an amazing storehouse of knowledge about fishing. She really could hire herself out as a guide. Her father had always told her she had a nose for where the fish would be biting.

"Daddy, look, it's that pretty house," Bethany exclaimed as they cruised around a bend.

Amanda realized she'd unconsciously headed for the Clooney mansion. When she was little, her father always made a point of rowing out this way so they could ogle the magnificent house.

"Former home of mayor Bill 'Possum' Clooney," Amanda said in her best tour-guide voice. "Clooney was a Dallas millionaire who decided he wanted to be a big fish in a little pond. He built this house back in the thirties, then tried to talk his friends into doing the same. I guess he thought it would be Dallas's version of the Hamptons, or something. But Cottonwood was too far from Dallas to be a convenient weekend destination, so the house has stood alone all these years. I guess it will forever be Cottonwood's biggest and grandest.''

''It looks bigger in person than it did in that picture on your bulletin board,'' Hudson said.

''I'm afraid no one will ever buy it. It's too pricey for this area.''

''I like this area. Very peaceful.''

''Most people just think of it as the sticks.''

''Do you like it here?''

''I love it here. I couldn't imagine living anyplace else. I love the slow pace of small-town life.''

Hudson laughed. ''You?''

She realized just how ridiculous that statement must have sounded to him. But she did love this town. Her own life might be fast-paced and unpredictable, but she could always count on Cottonwood and Town Lake staying the same.

''When I was little, my father used to tell me I was secretly a princess, and this house was my castle. But a dragon had chased me out. And someday he was going to slay the dragon, and we could all move back into the castle and wear velvet and satin and never do anything all day but eat bonbons—and fish, of course.''

''And did you believe him?'' Hudson asked quietly.

''I did for a little while. Then my mother told him to stop filling my head with nonsense. That's when I first realized we weren't really a royal family in exile." She laughed at her own gullibility. "I was pretty silly back then."

"Nothing silly about dreams. Do you think you'd still like to live there?"

"No," she said, a little too vehemently. "I want to sell it to someone else and get the commission." Abruptly she turned the boat away from the mansion, with its gleaming white brick and manicured lawns, and headed toward the good fishing spots she knew were right around the corner.

Finally she found it—one of her father's favorite haunts. She angled the boat into the small cove where conditions seemed perfect and cut the engine. Now, the fine art of choosing a lure. Hudson's old tackle box, which he'd found at the cabin, didn't have anything fancy, but it covered the basics. She chose a yellow spinner skirt for Hudson.

"Cast toward shore, then reel it in slowly," she instructed. "Let the lure hit bottom and slide from ledge to ledge."

She chose a classic Johnson Silver Minnow for herself, and finally, at Bethany's insistence, a hot pink frog for her, though Amanda secretly doubted the frog would catch anything, since it required a bit of skill on the angler's part.

She reviewed how to cast, keeping a careful eye on Bethany's hook as the little girl flailed around trying to imitate the adults.

"Let me help you until you get the hang of it," Amanda cautioned her. "Fish hooks can be very dangerous."

"I'll be careful," Bethany said solemnly.

Amazingly, Bethany's frog was the first to get a strike. She lost the first fish she hooked, but with Amanda's help she hooked the second one and got it safely into the boat—a nice two-pounder.

Amanda and Hudson soon caught their own fish. She really hadn't thought they would be so lucky. Once they had half a dozen largemouth in the live well, Bethany was more interested in watching them swim around in the small box than she was in catching more.

At precisely three forty-five, Amanda's watch alarm went off.

"What's that?" Hudson asked.

She punched the button on her watch. "That's a reminder that it's time to pack up. I didn't want to lose track of the time like I did the other day." And she had, she realized. Lazing in the sun with a line in the water had a way of contracting time. She could do it all day and not even notice the passage of the hours.

Hudson looked disappointed. "All right. You've been a pretty good sport about this."

"Well, it hasn't been such a sacrifice."

His eyes flared with interest, and she felt an answering response deep inside her chest. Was she flirting with Hudson? Yes, she was, and she didn't even regret it.

"You know, there are some other activities we can pursue to work on this blood pressure thing," she said as they both reeled their lines in. "If we get tired of fishing." Oh, yes, now she was definitely flirting. She was amazed she could still do it, she was so out of practice.

"Such as?"

*Massage.* She'd read in the booklet that massage was deeply relaxing. Instead she said, "Low-salt diet. Preparing meals from scratch is the only way to avoid salt, but it's so time consuming. So we could take turns."

"Or cook together. Then it would at least be more fun."

"Exercise. Fishing is relaxing, but it doesn't do much for the old cardiovascular system."

"Now who's sounding like a doctor?"

"I did some reading, that's all." Okay, in addition to reading the booklet, she'd spent two hours on the Internet last night downloading articles about blood pressure. She never did anything halfway. If it was worth doing, do it right. Blah, blah, blah. Sometimes she wished she could put a sock in that self-righteous internal voice that treated her to a nonstop monologue. "Oh, shoot, my line's hung up on something."

She tugged her pole this way and that, trying to get it loose from whatever the hook had grabbed on to. But it held fast, and she was beginning to think she would just have to cut the line and lose the lure.

She gave it one last, mighty tug—and it came loose. The lure flew through the air. Hudson's hands shot up in a reflexive gesture, shielding himself and Bethany from the flying hook. Unfortunately, the hook went right into his hand.

"Oh, jeez, son of a..." He cradled his injured hand, hook and all, against his chest.

"Oh, my God, did it get you?" Stupid question, she thought. Of course it got him, or he wouldn't be doing the dance of pain.

"What happened?" Bethany asked, her eyes huge.

"Your dad got a fish hook in his hand. I told you they could be dangerous."

"Did I do it?"

"No, baby, it was my fault."

"Do you think," Hudson said through gritted teeth, "that we could stop assessing blame and start doing something to fix this?" He opened his bloodied hand. The hook was deeply imbedded.

"Ewww!" Bethany said.

Amanda was a little lightheaded at the sight. She'd hooked herself in the arm once, when she was a girl, but there'd been hardly any blood and the hook had come right out.

"I think the thing to do," Amanda said, forcing herself to examine the wound more closely, "is to push the hook the rest of the way through, then clip off the barb."

AMANDA WAS PRACTICALLY talking surgery. The idea of undergoing such a procedure in the middle of the lake under these unsanitary conditions gave Hudson the heebie-jeebies. What he should do was wrap his hand in something to stop the bleeding, then go home to where he had a fully stocked doctor's bag and plenty of antiseptic.

But as he let Amanda gently probe the injury, he realized he enjoyed her ministrations. Besides, it would be hard to work on himself one-handed.

Amanda found a pair of wire cutters in the tackle box. She also discovered a first-aid kid on the boat, which included a small bottle of alcohol and some gauze. Hudson feigned ignorance about his treatment and let her take over. She might not be trained in the medical arts, but she had some common sense and a great bedside manner.

"Okay, this is going to sting." She poured some of the alcohol on to the wound. His hand caught fire, but Hudson found that if he focused his attention on where Amanda was lightly touching him, it didn't hurt as badly.

"Now I'm going to push the hook through. It doesn't have far to go, so it shouldn't be too bad. Take a deep breath."

He did, inhaling the vanilla scent of Amanda's silvery-blond hair. This close, he could see each individual strand—

"Ouch!"

"I'm sorry," she said, and he realized she was almost in tears. "That should be the worst of it."

The rest of the operation was accomplished quickly, though the injury was worse than Hudson had at first thought. What if he'd damaged the nerves in his hand? What if he couldn't perform surgery as a result?

That thought made him far more light-headed than the pain had.

Amanda wrapped his hand in enough gauze to outfit a mummy and taped it secure. By then her nearness had really gotten to him.

"Okay, all done," she said in a hoarse voice, making him wonder if she was as affected as he was.

When he looked into her clear blue eyes, which out here in the bright sun reminded him of aquamarine, he realized she was breathing hard.

It would be so easy, so natural, just to pull her those few extra inches closer and kiss her. Like falling off a log. And she wanted him to, if her moist, slightly parted lips and direct gaze were any indication.

He leaned closer. He was going to do it.

"Can we let the fish go now?" Bethany asked, oblivious to the sensual vibes coursing between Hudson and Amanda.

Amanda jerked back. "Yes, it's time to turn them loose," she said, sounding rattled.

Then she freed their captive bass, pulled up the anchor, started the boat and headed back to the marina. She didn't say a word.

"Did I make you late?" Hudson asked once she'd cut the motor. "Hell, you've got my blood all over you."

She looked down at her white cotton blouse, which had been liberally redecorated with red splotches. "Guess I'd better go home and change. It's okay, I don't have any appointments till five."

They said awkward goodbyes at the dock. Bethany, unusually quiet, didn't even extract a promise from Amanda about when they would get together again.

Hudson climbed into his rental car. "This won't be much fun for you, Bethany, but I'm going to the hospital."

"Didn't Amanda fix your hand?"

"She did a very good job. Most people aren't nearly so calm when there's an accident."

"Then why do you have to go to the hospital?"

"Because I want a nerve doctor to look at it. I have to be careful about my hands, since I'm a surgeon."

"Are you gonna die like Mommy?"

"Oh, sweetheart, no, of course not. This is a very minor injury. A little boo-boo," he amended, remembering he was talking to a four-year-old. "I just want to make sure it heals well, so my fingers will wiggle the way they're supposed to."

"There was a lot of blood."

"It looked worse than it was. Sometimes cuts bleed a lot."

"How will you get the blood back?"

"My body will make more. It's okay."

"Mommy lost too much blood and she died."

"Who told you that?" he asked, troubled that someone had been discussing her mother's death with her. He should be the one explaining, reassuring.

"No one. I saw it."

"But you couldn't remember. You weren't even three."

"I do remember. She had blood all down her face, and she had a sweater with a Christmas tree on it and it was all red, too."

*Oh, God.* Bethany did remember. That was exactly what Elaine had been wearing when she'd had the skiing accident. They'd brought her back to the lodge and she was waiting for an ambulance—dying—when she'd asked to see her daughter.

Hudson had been in a Zurich conference room, giving a speech. By the time he'd gotten word of the accident, it had been too late. He'd run into Charles

Kelso, one of Elaine's old boyfriends, at the hospital. He'd been covered in blood, too, and crying like a six-year-old. It hadn't taken Hudson long to figure out what had been going on.

"Do you remember any other times with Mommy?"

"I remember her hair. It was really long and I liked to play with it. And I remember we played with a white kitten."

Hudson was amazed. She'd only been three. The hair she could have gotten from photos, but the kitten had belonged to a neighbor at the house they'd lived in before Elaine's death.

"Think of Mommy that way—her hair, playing with the kitten. And, Bethany, I'm not going to die, okay?"

Bethany nodded, unusually solemn.

AMANDA TRIED TO FOCUS on work, but her thoughts kept returning to the afternoon's events. Maybe she shouldn't have tended to Hudson's injury herself. Maybe she should have just taken him straight to the hospital. But part of her had wanted to be his savior, his nurse, the one who made everything better. That was her grand role in life, to fix other people, if Margie could be believed.

But the hospital might have been overkill. What if he didn't have medical insurance? If he didn't have a job, that might be the case.

Other parts of the afternoon filled her thoughts, too—laughing with Hudson and Bethany over silly jokes she couldn't even remember, admiring Hudson's sexy body when she thought no one was watching...the almost kiss.

What was she thinking, flirting with someone like him? Number one, he would be leaving at the end of the month. Presumably he had a home in Boston. Number two, even if he wasn't a transient feature of her life, he was a bum! He was unemployed, but instead of looking for work, he was off playing with his daughter.

He seemed to be a concerned father, and she wouldn't fault him that. But the best, most responsible thing he could do for Bethany was to provide a good living for her. She would need clothes, books, a college education. Amanda was convinced the child was destined to be a zoologist.

He was so much like her father, it terrified her. Dan Dewhurst could have charmed the peel off an orange. But in the end he'd left his daughter with a host of unpleasant memories and wads of unpaid medical bills.

At five o'clock Margie found her sitting at her desk, her chin in her hand, staring into space.

"That must have been some fishing lesson."

"It was eventful. I snagged Hudson with a fishing hook and he almost bled to death."

Margie covered her gasp with her hand. "I wondered why you'd changed clothes. Was it fun otherwise?"

*Fun* wasn't the word Amanda would have used. *Stimulating,* perhaps.

"Your five-o'clock appointment is here."

Oh, hell, Amanda had forgotten all about them. She

should have printed out some likely listings for them to look at. "Stall them for about five minutes. Tell them I'm negotiating with a lender in California."

"Liar, liar, pants on fire," Margie said as she exited Amanda's office.

As soon as she finished with her clients, Amanda packed up her things and headed home. She was way behind, but she couldn't focus on her work until she checked on Hudson. She should remind him to get a tetanus booster.

When she got home, she saw that Mick's car was in the driveway. It was nice to see him home for a change. If he tried to slip out to the Red Dog Saloon she would—what *would* she do? Nag him about homework, like she had when he was a little kid? Take his car keys away? Those tactics didn't work anymore. She was just going to have to accept the fact that Mick didn't do things her way.

She found him in front of the TV, watching *Scooby-Doo*. "I always knew you were the intellectual type," she teased.

"Don't start with me, sis. I've had a hard day."

"Oh? And what exactly did you do during this 'hard day'?"

"Study."

"What did you study?"

"Business law. You know that class is eating my lunch."

She flipped through the day's mail as she grilled him. "Okay. Tell me one thing you learned about business law while studying today."

He rolled his eyes.

"I'm serious, Mick. If I'm paying for your college education, I'd like to know what you're learning."

"It's technical. You wouldn't understand it."

"Oh, because I didn't go to college? Because I'm just a dumb real estate agent?"

"I didn't say that."

She started to carry the argument further when an envelope from Tyler Junior College caught her eye. It was addressed to Michael Dewhurst.

She had a bad feeling about that envelope. She handed it to Mick. "It's for you."

He set it on the end table, his attention squarely on the TV.

"Open it."

He looked up at her, annoyed. "I'll get to it later."

"Open it now, or I will."

"Fine, go ahead, if you have that little trust in me." He stood and stalked to his bedroom.

Amanda wanted to trust him. But she couldn't, not after what Margie had told her. She ripped open the envelope and extracted the contents.

It was a check. A tuition refund. Mick had dropped both the classes he'd registered for.

"Studying, my Aunt Fanny!" she roared. Oh, hell, she had to get out of here before she did violence. She walked out the front door and, as she was standing out in the driveway, realized she had neither keys nor purse.

Then she spied the cabin next door. It lured her like a beacon. That was what she needed, the soothing balm of Bethany's laughter and Hudson's—no, it was the child, she told herself sternly. Hudson might be handsome as sin and charming as the devil, but his appeal was illusory. She told herself that over and over as her feet took her to Hudson's front door.

# Chapter Six

The front door was open. Amanda knocked on the wooden frame of the old screen door. "Hello. Anyone home?"

"I'm home!" Bethany sped to the door like a bullet and opened it. "Daddy's cooking!"

Judging from Bethany's level of surprise, this was not an everyday occurrence. Amanda stepped inside and around the corner to the kitchen, where she found Hudson laboriously chopping up celery with his left hand. His right hand hung at his side, useless.

He smiled sheepishly. "You made a good point about cooking from scratch."

"Great advice, for someone with two good hands. You don't fall into that category." She softened. "Does it hurt?"

"Not after that handful of aspirin I swallowed."

"You could probably use something stronger. And you should get a tetanus shot."

"I did. I, um, went to the hospital."

She gasped, and stepped closer, though she stopped before she actually touched him. They didn't know each other well enough for her to touch him spontaneously, and a comforting hug would probably be way out of line. "I didn't realize it was that bad."

"It wasn't. In fact, the doctor said you did an excellent job patching me up. But he thought a few stitches were in order."

"Twenty-four," Bethany piped in.

"Twenty-four stitches?" Amanda felt dizzy at the thought. "For a fish hook?"

"The doctor wanted to stitch up the muscle as well as the skin. He was worried I might lose some dexterity."

"Oh, Hudson, I'm so sorry. I should have been more careful. I should never have—"

"Hey, I'm the one who wanted to go fishing, remember? Relax. It's fine, and it hardly hurts at all. If you want to make it up to me, you'll stay for dinner."

"I'll do better than that." She took note of the pitiful pile of vegetables he'd chopped so far, and an unopened package of chicken breasts on the counter. "I think you need help."

"I can do this," he insisted.

"He's been chopping forever," Bethany said, "and I'm hungry."

Amanda washed her hands at the kitchen sink. "Stand aside and let an expert take over."

Hudson raised his eyebrows. "You cook? The Slimfast Queen?"

"Just because I choose not to cook now doesn't mean I don't know how. I cooked for my family from the time I was big enough to see over the stove. Mom worked long hours."

"And what about your dad?"

Amanda snorted her disdain. "Dad couldn't boil water."

"Don't be too scornful. That's about my skill level. I figured I could chop up stuff for salad and bake chicken breasts."

"I hate salad," Bethany added.

"How about we make stir-fry, then?" Amanda suggested. "You know, Chinese food?"

Bethany looked hopeful.

"Do you have rice?"

They had rice. Amanda put some on the stove, then made short work of the vegetables and chicken. In twenty-five minutes flat she had put an attractive meal on the table, even if she did say so herself. And she bet it would taste far better than Slimfast.

"Would your brother like to join us?" Hudson asked politely. "I noticed his car in the driveway."

"Mick can starve for all I care," Amanda snapped, then immediately regretted the outburst. She was sure Hudson and Bethany didn't want to hear about her family quarrels.

"Oooookay."

"Sorry." She gave him a rueful grin. "He's... misbehaving, that's all."

"Misbehaving? And how old is he?" Hudson asked skeptically.

"Twenty-two. Let's not talk about Mick, it'll spoil my appetite. Bethany, how is Shiny doing?"

"He's good. I'm gonna teach him tricks." She dived into the modest portion of stir-fry and rice Amanda had put on to her plate.

Hudson's jaw dropped. "It's a miracle."

"What?" Amanda asked.

"My child is eating vegetables."

"This isn't vegetables," Bethany corrected him. "It's rice and chicken and stuff."

"Have it your way."

Hudson and Amanda shared a secret smile, and somehow the day didn't seem like such a disaster anymore.

After a dessert of orange sherbet, Bethany helped Amanda clear and wash the dishes. Hudson put the dishes away as Bethany dried them—she did pretty well for such a little girl.

"So what shall we do now?" Hudson asked. "We could go for a walk in the woods, get some exercise."

"I'm not wearing the shoes for it," Amanda objected.

"So, go home and change."

She tried again. "I have a lot of work to catch up on." She'd already wasted more time today than was healthy for her career.

"Come with us. Please?" Bethany implored. "Please, please, please?"

Amanda could turn Hudson down, if she really worked at it. But she found it impossible to say no to Bethany's big brown eyes. "All right, a short walk."

She walked in her sandals, which were comfortable enough. She wasn't ready to face Mick yet.

They found a trail in the woods that was smooth and well-maintained. Bethany skipped ahead of them, chasing chipmunks and birds and squirrels, throwing pinecones, and generally having a good time being a kid. Amanda had to smile at her innocent high spirits.

She had been just like that, once upon a time, before she was old enough to realize she was dirt poor and her father was an irresponsible drunk.

"So what did Mick do that was so terrible?" Hudson asked.

"Oh, I don't want to talk about that."

"Maybe I could help. I was once a twenty-two-year-old male."

"Yes, but did you ever drop all your college courses, which your sister paid for, then pocket the tuition refund and pretend you were still enrolled?"

"Yikes."

"I don't know if it's an isolated incident, or if he's been doing it for four years. He never shows me his grades, but he seems to be going to class and writing papers and studying for tests. But he's also been hanging out every night at the Red Dog Saloon. And that's the worst of it, in my mind." She paused, then plunged ahead. Hudson would probably hear it from the town grapevine if not from her. "Our father was the town drunk. I don't want to see Mick go the same route."

"Does he work?"

"No. He's never even had a summer job. He always takes classes in the summer."

"But he hasn't graduated."

"He's changed majors a lot."

"I don't know how to tell you this, sweetheart, but you're being taken for a ride."

Amanda wanted to defend Mick. He was young. He was still finding his way. So he'd made mistakes. Didn't everybody? But the words wouldn't come, because she knew they were lies. Margie saw it, and

Hudson saw it, and she was just being a blind fool if she didn't admit the truth: Mick was taking advantage of her, and he had no intention of graduating or getting a job so long as she was footing the bill.

To her horror, her eyes filled with tears. She stopped, hoping to sniff them back before Hudson noticed, but no such luck.

"Are you crying?"

"N-no."

"Yes, you are." He glanced up ahead to see what Bethany was doing. She had stopped to play tightrope on a log. "Here, now, I'm sure it's not as bad as all that."

"M-my brother's a wastrel!"

Hudson enfolded Amanda in his arms, and she went willingly, as naturally as breathing. He felt warm and safe, and for just this little while she wanted someone to take care of her, for a change.

"He just hasn't grown up yet," Hudson soothed.

"He's been lying to me."

"And he got caught. So make sure he suffers the consequences."

"How?"

Hudson hesitated.

"You're not going to tell me to kick him out, are you? That's what Margie suggested. But you don't understand. He has no money of his own. No place to go. He'll end up a street person."

"Even if that's true, which I doubt, you can't live his life for him. He's a grown man. Let him make his choices and live with them."

"But that would be like quitting, giving up. Losing."

"And you don't like to lose. Oh, Amanda, I've got you all figured out."

She looked up at him, surprised by his words. "How could you? You barely know me."

"Because you're my reflection."

"What does that mean?"

Instead of answering, he kissed her. At first it was just a quick graze of his lips against hers. Then he searched her face, perhaps waiting for some indication—a nod or a yes or the slight tilt of her chin—that meant she was on the same page as he was.

And was she? Did she want him to kiss her?

Yes, she was afraid she did. But with her acquiescence, would she be starting down a path she might regret? Sure, he was big and strong and sexy and comforting right now. But in the long run—

"Would you just stop weighing the pros and cons of whether this is a smart move or not? It's just a kiss."

She licked her lips, then thought, *What the hell. It's just a kiss.*

He wasted no time taking advantage of her agreement, leaning down and claiming her mouth with his. She sucked in a breath as nerve endings all over her body vibrated with the slight contact. Before she could even get an inkling that this might not be like other kisses she'd experienced, he deepened the kiss, angling his mouth on hers and staking his claim.

She touched his tongue with hers, tentatively at first, then more boldly as a comforting warmth spread from her chest outward, making her feel as if she might fall if he didn't have his arms around her, one hand at the back of her head.

"Daddy, I found a frog!"

At the sound of Bethany's excited squeal, Amanda drew back, slightly panicked. They shouldn't be kissing like this in front of a child. But Hudson, apparently not troubled at all, just grinned.

"She's not even watching us."

"Still…"

Reluctantly he released her, though he threw an arm around her waist. "C'mon, let's have a look at that frog."

Amanda realized part of her hair had fallen from the confines of the dozen or so pins she used to put it up every morning. She started to repair the damage, but Hudson stilled her hands with his.

"Leave it. It looks good."

"My hair looks good half falling down?"

He gave it a critical examination, making her want to squirm. Then he reached up and pulled a few more pins out, and the rest of the heavy mass of her hair fell past her shoulders.

"There." He pocketed the pins so she couldn't fix it, then went to see what Bethany had found.

HUDSON COULDN'T STOP sneaking glances at Amanda. She had been pretty before, but with her thick, silver-blond hair hanging in iridescent waves halfway down her back, she was an erotic image, a pagan goddess, maybe the goddess of sex, if there was such a thing. He couldn't remember the last time he'd been so captivated by a woman, especially one who seemed so unaware of her desirability. He wanted to kiss her again, deeper, longer, to drag her to his bed and make love to her for hours on end.

The intensity of his fantasies surprised him. He'd always considered himself above such base instincts. But maybe he'd never been tempted to such a degree before.

After their walk, Amanda again made noises about going home and finishing her work, but Bethany dragged out an old game of Monopoly she'd found in a closet. She was really too young to understand much about the game, but she could roll the die and count spaces around the board, and she understood amassing large quantities of cash.

"Grandma Ruth always has a big roll of money in her purse," Bethany said as she counted her pile of ones. "She doesn't trust the bank."

What Ruth Hanover didn't trust was ATM machines. But Hudson didn't elaborate on Bethany's observation. Amanda would probably think Bethany's grandmother was some ignorant hillbilly who kept all her savings stuffed in a mattress, and that was fine with him. He still hadn't gotten over the novelty of people not knowing he was a wealthy doctor.

The bank ran out of money before they finished the game, but that was okay. It was Bethany's bedtime, and he was more than anxious to have his delectable neighbor all to himself. For the past hour he'd been brushing hands with Amanda, inhaling her scent, watching her moist, pink mouth as she talked and laughed, and he had just about reached his limit. He either had to do something about his sudden, all-encompassing desire for her, or take a cold shower.

Bethany made only a token objection to going to bed. She was tired after the active day, and her eyes were already drooping by the time he got her tucked into her bed in the sleeping loft.

"Is Amanda going to spend the night?" she asked innocently.

He wished. "No, sweetie, she has to go home to her own house."

"I wish she could live with us."

"Well, that's not going to happen."

"She'd make a good mommy."

He couldn't argue with Bethany there. Amanda might not have much experience with kids, but she was a natural with this one, anyway. "What about Janey?" he asked, whispering so there was no chance Amanda would overhear. "Wouldn't she make a good mommy?"

"Janey's pretty," Bethany said. "But she doesn't fish or play games with me."

The very idea of Janey fishing, or pushing a metal dog around a Monopoly board, made Hudson want to burst out laughing. "But she takes you shopping, and to Godiva Chocolates, and she lets you try on her jewelry."

"Yeah," Bethany said on a nod. "Janey's nice. I miss Janey and Grandma Ruth and Grandma Judith."

Good, Hudson thought. Because Janey was probably who he would end up marrying. Which was a sane enough reason to forget about Amanda Dewhurst. He should never even have kissed her, since he was quasi-engaged to another woman.

AMANDA WAITED AWKWARDLY in the kitchen. Since she abhorred idle hands, she'd scrubbed the ancient porcelain sink, sponged the refrigerator door and wiped down counters that had already been cleaned. When Hudson finally reappeared, she was wrapping up the garbage to take to the street.

"You don't have to do that," Hudson objected.

"I was just killing time. Garbage pickup is tomorrow morning, you know."

"No, I didn't know."

"I really should be going."

"But you don't want to. I can tell."

"I don't want to face Mick. No, that's not all of it," she added quickly. "I don't want to leave you. I've had a really good time tonight. Thank you for inviting me to stay. For dinner, I mean." Oh, hell, now he'd think she wanted him to ask her to stay the night.

Which she did. And if he asked, she would say yes. She'd found a safe little haven here with Hudson and Bethany, a place where she didn't have to think about listings and the new FHA requirements and whether it was time to change her oil or her air-conditioning filters. Here she didn't have to be Amanda Dewhurst, responsible daughter, sister, homeowner and real estate agent. She could just be…well, she could just *be*.

He stared at her intently. She met his gaze for a few seconds, then had to look away. Why was he looking at her that way? Like a kid looking through a toy store window at a model train he couldn't afford.

"Your financial status doesn't matter to me," she blurted out.

"What?" Then he looked away, his face moving into harsh lines. "Oh, I see. You know, then."

"I know only what you've told me. But I can guess. You feel like maybe you shouldn't get involved with me because you don't have a job and you don't know where you'll be come the end of the month."

He looked back at her quickly. Clearly that wasn't what he had expected her to say. "I do know where I'll be in a month. I have to go home and try to put things back together."

She digested this for a few moments. "Is Bethany's mother waiting there for you?" She might as well find out the worst.

A shadow crossed Hudson's face. "Bethany's mother died about two years ago."

Amanda wanted to bite her tongue off. "Now it's my turn to say I'm sorry for speaking before thinking."

"I'm not still grieving. That's not why I came here."

"Then what did bring you here?"

He shrugged. "I needed to make a change. Things in Boston weren't working. Sometimes you just have to shake things up, you know?"

Boy, did she know. Alarm bells went off in her head. How many times had her father used almost those exact words when trying to explain to his family why he quit yet another job, or why they had to move, or why he'd done any number of crazy things when he'd had a few too many?

This was crazy. Hudson Stack wasn't someone she needed to get involved with. He wasn't a bad person. But neither did words like *responsible, ambitious* or *hardworking* come to mind. And those were qualities she would insist on with any man who wanted to partner with her, even in the short term. His bank account didn't bother her, but his lack of ambition did. She wasn't about to fall in love with a man's potential or his good intentions. What she wanted, needed, in a man was a work ethic. Otherwise, how would he ever understand her own goal-oriented lifestyle?

"I really should go."

"How many times are you going to say that?"

"Until I convince myself to follow through, I guess."

"What are you going to tell Mick?"

Ugh. She'd managed to forget about him for a couple of hours. "I'll think of something. I always do."

"I like you, Amanda. I also want you. I guess that's no big surprise. But maybe it would be better if we didn't go there."

She nodded. "Much wiser."

"Good night, then."

"Yes, good night." She turned, got as far as the door, actually had her hand on the knob when she turned to look at him one more time.

The naked hunger she saw in his eyes did her in. No man had ever looked at her like that, like he was dying of starvation and she was the last morsel of bread on earth.

Somehow the distance between them closed. She didn't remember how she got there, only that she was in Hudson's arms, and he was kissing her mouth and her face and burrowing into her hair with his fingers and pressing the hard length of his body against hers. She registered a thousand sensations at once—the feel of his hands, the raspy sound of his breath, the scent of his skin, an intoxicating blend of shaving cream and leather and fresh air and sunshine. And the tinglings in her own body, little voices calling out from everywhere at once begging for attention, for fulfillment, for release.

She was impaled on the sword of her own desire, which she could no more deny than she could stop breathing.

If he would have her.

"Bedroom," he managed.

Okay, that answered that question. She waited for him to lead the way, but instead he scooped her into his arms like some medieval knight claiming a swooning maiden.

And she was swooning, she decided, now fully appreciating the meaning of the word. She closed her eyes and didn't open them again until she was lying on Hudson's bed.

## Chapter Seven

The room was dark, but Hudson didn't need to see. He could feel Amanda, sense her, home in on her warmth and her desire for him, a welcome and palpable entity. He even managed to forget the throbbing of his injured hand.

He wanted to consume her. He'd never felt anything like this, wasn't sure he could control it. He'd always been wary of things he couldn't control, but nothing was going to stop him now. Nothing short of an objection from Amanda.

He lay down beside her, threw one possessive leg over her as if to stop her from escaping, then resumed the steamy kisses that had brought them here in the first place.

From somewhere he found the courage to halt the kisses long enough to say, "Stop me if I'm going too fast."

"I don't think that's possible."

Her words inflamed him. He felt an uncommon impatience to see her body naked, to touch her, to join with her.

No more words were necessary; she understood. He

literally trembled with anticipation as he unbuttoned her oh-so-sensible cotton blouse, then plunged his hands inside and filled his palms with her breasts encased in a soft, satiny bra.

Amanda welcomed his tongue as he probed deeply into the cavern of her mouth, and it was all he could do to contain his passion. Where was it coming from? The intensity of his desire was almost a third being in the room with them, pushing his hands to caress and gently squeeze and to suck on her full lower lip, kissing in a way he'd never kissed any woman before.

The feel of that slippery satin against her skin, the clean smell of soap and the light scent that clung to her hair, wound their way around his senses like a jungle vine, gradually tightening their hold on him until he was nearly mindless.

He shifted his weight and moved his hands to her bottom, fitting the cradle of her hips against him. Though they were still fully clothed below the waist, the contact felt overwhelmingly intimate. He wanted Amanda to feel how hard he was and to know that she was the reason.

Amanda broke the kiss long enough to get his shirt unbuttoned. Then she pressed her face against his chest, circling one nipple with her tongue. He shuddered and groaned, wondering if she had any idea how thoroughly she was torturing him, but he certainly didn't want her to stop.

She undid his belt and the buttons on his jeans, then reached inside and stroked his arousal. He wouldn't have guessed her to be that bold. Outwardly she seemed like she might be more fussy about her lovemaking, more prim. But apparently he'd unleashed something wild in her.

''Amanda,'' he said on a groan. ''Too much.''

She didn't seem to hear him. He was far too close to the finish line, and he sure as hell didn't want to be out here in the cold when he crossed it. He grabbed her hand and stilled her efforts. ''Give me half a chance here.'' He felt rather than saw her embarrassed smile.

Slow, sweet seduction was for another time. Now he just wanted her naked. Maybe he was a little rough, but she didn't complain as he pulled her clothes off and flung them all over the room.

Soon nothing separated their bodies.

Hudson was so turned on he was half out of his mind. Still worried he might hurt her in his rush to join with her, he rolled to his back and pulled her on top of him.

She had no problem with that. She straddled him, brushing her velvet softness against him, flirting with penetration and then pulling back. Was it fear that made her tremble and fueled her hesitation?

''We can take it slower if you want,'' he whispered, his face buried against her neck.

''No. I was just…anticipating.''

''Teasing?''

''No, I didn't mean to be—''

''Stop worrying.'' He silenced her needless apology with another searing kiss, then grasped her hips and brought them downward, plunging into her hot, wet depths.

Nothing had ever felt sweeter. She rode him hard,

rising above him, then sheathing him again and again in a frenzied rhythm. In the darkness all he could make out was that incredible cloud of hair around her head, haloing her like an angel. A very, very naughty angel.

The sensual dance lasted longer than seemed possible until, unable to hold back, Hudson exploded inside her. Mindlessly he fell into a black velvet of pure pleasure. She cried out and followed him to some place where they seemed to be together, but on another plain of existence. Afterward he would swear, at least to himself, he'd had an out-of-body experience. Then she slumped against him.

Her face was damp, from sweat, he hoped. If she was crying, he wasn't sure he could handle it.

They lay together for a long time, breathing in harmony, truly one in body and soul. Then she took his bandaged hand and kissed it gently. "Still hurt?"

"Not at all. It's a miracle."

A few minutes later, or maybe it was hours, Hudson decided the room was too dark. He slipped out of Amanda's light, drowsy embrace, walked to the window and threw open the blinds. Moonlight flooded in, reflecting in her hair and on her skin, which glowed like alabaster. The curve of her cheek and the moist cherry of her well-kissed mouth caused his libido to stir again. This need for Amanda was like a thirst that couldn't be slaked.

"What are you doing?" she asked, rousing slightly from her sex-induced stupor.

"Letting in some light. I should have done this earlier. I like to see a woman when I'm making love to her."

She crossed her arms over her breasts. "You could turn on a lamp instead. What if someone looks in?"

Instead of reasoning with her, a battle he was sure to lose, he lay down beside her again and caressed her face. "Let them look. You were made for moonlight."

She smiled. "That's the most romantic thing anyone's ever said to me."

It was probably the most romantic thing he'd ever said. He wasn't the kind of guy who sent flowers and candy or showered women with expensive perfume or effusive compliments. He considered that old-fashioned, and none of his girlfriends from the past, or his wife, had demanded it or even seemed to expect it.

But suddenly he felt as if he wanted to do all kinds of romantic things for Amanda.

"Will you stay?" he asked.

"That's not a very good example to set for Bethany."

Bethany. As usual, he wasn't putting his daughter first, only his own selfish needs.

"Stay a while, then. I want to make love to you again. Slower."

He knew the moment her mood shifted. Her face stiffened, and the tension he was used to seeing there returned. "I've got to go home. This is insane."

"A little bit," he agreed. "It's also normal, natural behavior for two consenting adults who are attracted to each other."

"We hardly know each other."

"Are you going to worry this to death?"

She flashed a rueful smile. "Probably. That's what I do best."

"Well, stop it. Your blood pressure, remember?"

She sighed.

"We could do a test. Measure it before—" he kissed her warmly "—then after." He kissed her again.

She wiggled away from his embrace. "Enough, really. This is enough insanity for one evening. I need to regroup."

"You mean you need to go home, think about it obsessively and decide it was a bad idea."

She blinked in surprise. "You do have me figured out."

"Only because I know myself. Once you're out of sight, out of my reach, I'll probably do the same thing. Which is a good reason, in my humble opinion, for you to stay right here."

He kissed her several more times. She gradually relaxed again under his ministrations, until all at once she sat bolt upright. "Hudson, we didn't use any— Oh, holy cow."

Hudson froze. "We didn't? You're not—"

"Why would I be? I haven't had a date in three years. And I can't believe I just admitted that to you." She covered her face with her hands.

Hudson was less concerned with her embarrassment than with the risk they'd just taken. It hadn't even crossed his mind. Though he'd dated no one but Janey since Elaine—and they hadn't slept together—he'd had his share of liaisons before. And always the woman had taken care of protection. In fact, most every woman he knew took the birth control injections so she didn't have to worry about it.

"I guess I was a total jerk for expecting you to take care of it."

She groaned. "How could we be so dumb?"

"Do the words *carried away* mean anything to you? It does happen."

"Not to me, it doesn't." She got up and searched for her clothes.

"For what it's worth, if anything were to…happen, I would take responsibility."

"That doesn't really ease my mind."

He should tell her. He should let her know that if she were to have his child, the child would never want for anything. In fact, she'd probably never have to work another day in her life. It might be the best thing that could happen to her.

He was about to spill the beans when she said something that changed his mind. "The last thing you need, Hudson, is another mouth to feed. We're probably worrying for nothing. But if there's really something to worry about, it'll be my responsibility."

As she finished buttoning her blouse, she leaned over the bed and kissed him quickly. "I really have to go."

"Wait." His mind raced as he struggled to think of something that would keep her here, or something that guaranteed he would see her again. "When's our next fishing lesson?"

She got a pained expression on her face. "I know I promised but…"

"You don't want to? You mean, this is it?"

"I'm confused."

"I think you're confused because it's been so long since you had any fun, you don't know how to handle it. For some reason, you don't feel like you deserve to relax and enjoy yourself. Or to have an occasional lapse in judgment."

"I don't need this," she said, drawing self-righteous indignation around her like a cloak. "If I wanted to be analyzed, I'd go to a psychiatrist."

"But you *do* need it. That's the point."

"Why do you feel like you have to save me?"

That was a good question, and one he didn't have an answer for.

AMANDA PICKED HER WAY from the cabin to her house aided only by moonlight, wondering what the hell was going on. She'd just had unprotected sex with a man she hardly knew. She'd been away from her cell phone for hours on end, though she'd told several people she would be available tonight.

Mick wasn't home, and for once she was grateful. He was probably afraid to face her, and well he should be. She was going to take off his head when she saw him again.

She pulled her cell phone out of her purse and checked for messages. She had only one, thank goodness. She grabbed a pen and listened. It was from a man she'd shown some houses to that morning. He'd seemed reserved and unenthusiastic, and she'd figured she would never see him again. She was surprised to hear his voice.

"Listen, Amanda, I'd like to make an offer on that

first house we saw, the one on Cherry. Give me a call ASAP, because I have to be on a plane tomorrow morning at six.''

Amanda let loose a string of curses that turned the air around her blue. While she'd been lollygagging next door, a sale had been slipping through her fingers. She might salvage it. She'd worked out many a deal with faxes and e-mails and earnest money FedExed to her office. But by the time she caught up with the guy, he might have seen another property he liked better, or his wife might have talked him out of it.

This was what happened when she let her attention waver, even for a minute. She had to do a better job of keeping her eye on her goals. And that meant steering clear of Hudson Stack and his adorable daughter.

There was still the matter of the fishing lessons she'd promised. But after what had happened, she just didn't see how she could spend so much time with Hudson. Now that she knew what his hands felt like on her body, she could never keep him at arm's distance again. Now that his kiss was forever etched into her memory, she would be wanting him to kiss her every time she saw him. She knew what he looked like naked, and she would never be able to look at him clothed again without thinking of his smooth, warm skin, the intricate play of muscles in his back, his flat stomach, the way his hair-roughened legs felt intertwining with hers—

*Stop it!* She was just going to get herself all worked up again, and there was no good in that. She took a quick shower to thoroughly rid herself of his scent, threw her clothes in the washing machine and went to bed.

Sleep didn't come easily. She'd given her word, her promise. And there was the matter of her blood pressure. Fishing was supposed to lower it. But worrying about Hudson Stack was making it go higher, she was sure. What was she going to do? What if she was pregnant? What if Mick ended up as a street person? What if an earthquake swallowed the whole state of Texas?

She groaned and pulled her pillow over her head.

Amanda had finally gotten to sleep when a door slamming shut woke her up. Mick. Damn it, another reason to be mad at him. Now she would toss and turn for another hour before she finally found some peace in the sweet oblivion of sleep.

The stairs creaked, and she heard female giggling and whispering. What the hell? Who was in her house? And why were they coming up here to the loft, which was her private domain?

She grabbed a heavy real-estate-law book from the floor and prepared to do battle.

Someone knocked softly on her door. "Sis? Are you awake?"

Amanda slumped against the pillows, relieved and surprised that Mick would seek her out. "I am now," she groused. "Come in."

He opened the door and stepped inside. Amanda switched on the bedside lamp. Tonya Green was with him, grinning from ear to ear.

"We didn't wake you, did we?" Tonya asked.

"No. I'm always wide awake when I'm in my

nightgown in bed with the lights off at two in the morning.''

''Oh, good,'' Tonya said, the sarcasm going right over her head.

''We're sorry to bother you so late,'' Mick said with uncharacteristic politeness, ''but we just couldn't wait to tell you the good news. We're getting married!''

Amanda had barely absorbed that shocking tidbit when Tonya added insult to injury. ''And you're going to be an aunt!''

AMANDA GOT HER THIRD CUP of sludge from the office coffee maker, hoping it might improve her outlook or at least her level of alertness. After Mick's startling news, she'd gotten maybe three hours of sleep. Though she'd managed to hold it together long enough to get the happy couple out of her room, and had even managed a smile and some form of congratulations, she'd lain awake most of the night, wondering how on earth she was going to head off this latest disaster.

Mick, married with a wife and child? The thought was ludicrous. She probably would have said so, if not for the baby. Mick was in no way ready for the marriage. But he'd gotten a girl pregnant, he was ready and willing to do the right thing and she wasn't going to discourage him.

On the other hand, if she didn't do something, she could see an unpleasant future stretching out endlessly before her. Tonya would move in with her and Mick. Tonya would have to quit work when her pregnancy advanced. Then she would have a baby, and Amanda would be supporting all four of them and probably taking care of the baby every evening while Mick and Tonya were out dancing at the Red Dog Saloon.

Maybe supporting five, if she was pregnant herself. It was only a small chance, but she couldn't stop thinking about it. She couldn't rely on Hudson for much in the way of support. A maintenance man, a single parent trying to raise one child already wouldn't have much disposable income to toss her way, and she wouldn't burden him that way, anyway.

She didn't suppose he would want to marry her. And even if he did—well, shoot, she could support seven as well as five, right? She would just have to sell a few more houses.

"You look like you're contemplating murder."

Amanda jumped. She'd been standing in front of the coffee pot, poised to fill her cup, for who knew how long as she'd lost herself in her unpleasant fantasy.

"Contemplating suicide, more like it," she said as she put cream and sugar in her coffee.

Margie took the pot from her and filled her own cup. "Did Mr. Murphy get hold of you last night?"

"No. I left a message for him this morning."

"You didn't talk to him?" Margie was surprised.

"No. I had my phone turned off."

"I thought you were going to be home last night."

"Well, for once I wasn't, okay?"

Margie recoiled. "Sorry." She tiptoed back toward the front desk.

"Oh, Margie, I'm sorry. I'm such a doofus. I don't mean to growl at you. It's just that my life seems to be hurtling out of control. Mick's been lying to me about school, he's gotten Tonya Green pregnant, and he wants to marry her, and I might be pregnant, too.''

Margie froze halfway to sitting down. Her jaw dropped. ''Who's pregnant?''

''Tonya Green.''

''Oh. For a minute I thought you said you might be.'' And she laughed. Uproariously.

''Is it so unbelievable I could be pregnant?''

''When you haven't had a date in, what, five years?''

''Three. Don't make it worse than it is. Remember, I went out with—''

''Don't distract me.'' Margie lowered her voice. ''You aren't pregnant, are you?''

Amanda blew out a breath. ''Probably not.''

''But you could be? Who'd you do the dirty with? Oh, my stars, you don't have to tell me. Hudson Stack. Oh, honey, no one could blame you. Now that the Hardison boys are all married, he's the best-looking bachelor in town.''

''How'd you know it was him?''

''Unless it was bald, jowly Mr. Murphy. You haven't been seen with any other men.'' Margie looked as if she wanted to burst with this news.

''Margie, you can't tell anybody.''

Margie's smile faded. ''Oh, shoot, you kill all my fun. Can I tell people about Mick and Tonya?''

''Yes, I think they're going public today.''

''Okay, leave me alone. I have phone calls to make.''

Amanda retreated into her office. Her month was

off to a terrible start, and it was all Hudson's fault. Okay, it was her own fault, for falling prey to Hudson's charms. If her life was spinning out of control, she was at least partly responsible. And starting here and now, she was going to fix it.

She would start with Mick. Tonight she would have a serious talk with him. She would tell him that Tonya could not move in with them when he married her, that he would have to find his own place. And no, she wouldn't pay the rent on an apartment. He would have to get a job. She would encourage him to continue his education, and she would offer to pay tuition, but he would otherwise have to support himself.

She felt better just having made the decision.

The morning went well after that. Mr. Murphy returned her call. He really did want the house, and he faxed an offer to her. It was a good offer, and when she contacted the sellers, they made a good counter. She was confident the deal would go through.

She barreled through her paperwork, contacting two people who'd listed their house for sale by owner. Mary Jo had gotten to one of the owners first and had apparently irritated the couple, because they hung up on Amanda. But the second one agreed to let her come by and do a Comprehensive Market Analysis to determine if he was asking the right price. By the time she was done being helpful and supportive and not pressuring him to sign with Tri-County Realty, he would be eating out of her hand.

She designed a new flyer to distribute for a house she'd just listed and got it off to the printer.

"Okay, I'm back on track," she told herself over

and over, murmuring the sentence like a mantra. As she was heading out to an open house, a woman coming through the door nearly ran her over. It took a moment to realize the woman was Tonya.

"Oh, Amanda, just the person I wanted to see."

"I'm on my way somewhere," Amanda said, because she didn't want to talk to Tonya until she had her emotions under better control. It wasn't Tonya's fault she'd fallen victim to Mick's charms. Mick was his father's son, after all.

"I just wanted to thank you," Tonya said quickly. "I was afraid you'd go ballistic when you found out about the baby, but Mick said you'd be cool—not like my parents."

Tonya looked down at her feet.

Amanda couldn't help herself. She felt her heart going out to the clueless Tonya. "They didn't take the news well?"

"Not too well. Actually, they kicked me out."

Oh, great. *Here it comes,* Amanda thought.

"I've been living in my car for a couple of days. Mick said I could move in with y'all, but I wanted to ask you first. It is your house and all."

Shoot, shoot, shoot! How was Amanda supposed to tell this poor pregnant girl that she had to continue sleeping in her car?

"Of course you can move in with us," Amanda found herself saying.

Tonya hugged her. "Oh, thank you, thank you. You won't regret it. Once I get another job, I'll pay rent and help with the housework and everything!"

"You don't…have a job?"

# Get FREE BOOKS and a FREE GIFT when you play the...

# LAS VEGAS

## GAME

*Just scratch off the gold box with a coin. Then check below to see the gifts you get!*

## YES! I have scratched off the gold Box. Please send me my 2 FREE BOOKS and gift for which I qualify. I understand that I am under no obligation to purchase any books as explained on the back of this card.

▼ DETACH AND MAIL CARD TODAY! ▼

### 354 HDL DUYM          154 HDL DUY3

| | |
|---|---|
| FIRST NAME | LAST NAME |

ADDRESS

| | |
|---|---|
| APT.# | CITY |

STATE/PROV.          ZIP/POSTAL CODE          (H-AR-04/03)

| | | | |
|---|---|---|---|
| 7 | 7 | 7 | Worth TWO FREE BOOKS plus a BONUS Mystery Gift! |
| 🍒 | 🍒 | 🍒 | Worth TWO FREE BOOKS! |
| 🔔 | 🔔 | ♣ | TRY AGAIN! |

Visit us online at
www.eHarlequin.com

Offer limited to one per household and not valid to current Harlequin American Romance® subscribers. All orders subject to approval.

© 2001 HARLEQUIN ENTERPRISES LTD.
® and TM are trademarks owned by Harlequin Enterprises Ltd.

"I got fired last week. But I've been interviewing lots and I'm sure I'll have another job soon."

Amanda felt the blood draining from her head. "I'm sure you will, too. I always thought you made the prettiest cones at DQ."

Tonya smiled as if Amanda had just given her a diamond.

## Chapter Eight

It soon became obvious to Hudson that Amanda was avoiding him. She left her house before sunrise every morning and got home late at night.

Mick and Tonya seemed to be spending a lot of time at the house, however. One afternoon while Hudson and Bethany were planting some petunias he'd bought at Garden City, the young couple drove up in a pick-up truck filled with boxes, which they hauled inside. It appeared Tonya was moving in.

Hudson just shook his head and tried to forgive Amanda for ignoring him. It looked as if she had something else to worry about.

He gave her four days, and then he'd had enough. He went to her office right after lunch and waited for her. Having been the victim of stalking females before, Hudson wasn't thrilled with his behavior. But Amanda owed him something. If she was no longer interested now that they'd made love, he wanted to hear it from her own lips. At least if she made a clean break, he could get on with his life and the business of trying to forget her.

In about a hundred years.

As he sat in one of the uncomfortable chairs in the waiting room flipping through a decorating magazine that bored him silly, Margie watched him with undisguised curiosity.

Margie reached for the phone.

"Don't you dare call her and tell her I'm here," he said, anticipating Margie. "She'll never come back."

Margie *tsked* sympathetically. "She's giving you the runaround, huh?"

"To put it mildly."

"What's the runaround?" Bethany asked.

Sometimes the child's questions drove him nuts. She wasn't content to just play in her own world, the way a lot of children were. She listened intently to the adults almost all the time and insisted on understanding what they were talking about.

"The runaround is when you avoid seeing someone," Hudson explained, "or you make excuses for why you can't see them or talk to them."

"And Amanda's doing that?" Bethany looked surprised. "Is she mad at us?"

"Not at you, sweetheart," Hudson reassured her. "And she's not really mad. It's just that she has a busy life, and she seems to think she doesn't have extra time to spend with us."

"Why does she have to work so much?"

"The same reason most people do, I guess. She has to make money to buy food and pay for her house and gas for her car and clothes to wear."

"But, Daddy, you have lots of money," Bethany whispered, because her grandmothers had both taught her it was gauche to talk in public about how rich they were. "Why do you have to work so hard?"

"I work hard for different reasons. I work hard because there's no one else who can do what I do, and people need me to fix their hearts."

"Why don't we give Amanda some money, and then she wouldn't have to work so hard?"

Pretty good logic for a four-year-old, and it was a tempting thought. But if Amanda was the type of woman he could buy, then she'd be like the dozens of other females who'd come after him in recent weeks, and he wouldn't be so drawn to her.

Still, he couldn't help wondering if she might relax a bit if she got ahead financially.

His gaze fell on the bulletin board, and the picture of the Clooney mansion jumped out at him. That was it. The perfect solution. He stood suddenly.

"We have to go."

Margie looked distressed. "She'll be back anytime. Don't give up on her."

"I haven't given up. Tell her we stopped by."

"Where are we going, Daddy?" Bethany asked as he practically dragged her out the door.

"Remember that huge house we saw when we went fishing?"

Bethany's eyes lit up. "The one in the picture."

"We're going to buy it."

Of course, the matter would have to be accomplished with the utmost secrecy. As soon as they got in the car, Hudson took out his cell phone and called his business manager, Arthur Wright, giving him explicit instruction for how to conduct the purchase.

"Wait a minute," Arthur said. "You're telling me to pay the asking price for this house? You don't want to haggle at all?"

"That's right."

"And you're not actually planning to live in this house?"

"Nope."

"Is it some kind of great investment?"

"It seems reasonably priced."

Arthur sounded more and more confused. "Are you going to rent it out?"

"Actually, I'll probably just turn around and sell it."

"You want to explain?"

"No. Just be sure you work with Amanda Dewhurst, no one else. And under no circumstances mention my name."

"You've gone completely over the edge, haven't you?"

"You might say that," Hudson replied with a laugh. "Anything else going on I should know about?"

"Before you left, you told me not to keep you informed. You didn't want to have to worry about financial things."

"As long as I'm still solvent."

"All right, nothing financial, then. But your mother's been driving me crazy, wanting to know exactly where you are. And Janey. They're worried about you, and no amount of reassurances from me will convince them you're okay."

Ah, hell. Just thinking about his mother made his chest feel tight. And Janey…Janey made him feel guilty. Though they'd never defined their relationship as exclusive, in practice he hadn't gone out with anyone else, and he was pretty sure she hadn't, either.

"I'll call them right now," Hudson promised. But somehow, he managed to put off the phone calls.

ONE WEEK LATER Amanda's hands shook as she opened the FedEx package from Boston. Sure enough, there was a cashier's check for almost a million dollars, of which roughly twenty thousand dollars would be hers to keep. Lord, she'd never seen so many zeroes on a check!

This deal had come out of the blue. She had no idea how the anonymous buyer had come across her name. But without even lifting a finger, she'd sold him the Clooney mansion, and the buyer hadn't even argued about the price.

And he'd paid cash.

She examined the signed contract. Everything appeared to be in order.

Margie stared over Amanda's shoulder. "I can't believe this. In all my years in this business, I've never seen anything like it."

"I guess my guardian angel is watching over me."

"What are you going to do with the money?" Margie asked.

"That's easy. Pay off the Lincoln. Without that car payment to sweat every month, life will be so much easier."

"Will it?" Margie asked. "Will you actually relax a bit?"

Amanda sighed. "I need to. You know what really

bites, though? The Clooney mansion is Mary Jo's listing. This won't put me ahead of her at all.''

Margie sighed with exasperation. ''Will you forget Mary Jo?''

She wanted to. Amanda was a good agent, she earned lots of money for the company, and Jerry was ecstatic with her performance. She should be satisfied with that and not worry about whether Mary Jo got to keep the stupid trophy on her desk. But she still felt if she let down her guard, even for an instant, it would all cave in on her like a house of cards.

''Amanda, this competitive streak of yours has gotten out of hand.''

Amanda bit her lip. ''That bad?''

''Couldn't you at least forget about beating Mary Jo for the rest of the month? That's only two weeks. Rest on your laurels. Treat yourself to some nice things, like a massage and a manicure. Let Mary Jo have the trophy this month.''

''Let Mary Jo have the trophy?'' Amanda heard the screech in her own voice and took a deep breath to calm down.

''It would mean a lot to her. Maybe if she beat you once, she'd get it out of her system. And the two of you could play nice.''

''You really think so?''

''And you could try to repair the damage you've done to your neighbor,'' Margie added, not meeting Amanda's eyes.

Amanda felt an immediate stab of guilt. She'd behaved pretty horribly. If a guy slept with her and immediately dumped her the way she had Hudson, she would consider him a cad and worse. But he scared her. The way she acted around him scared the *hell* out of her.

"He's the best thing to happen to you in years," Margie said softly. "If you don't do something, some other woman is going to steal him out from under your nose."

"Look, Margie. He's gorgeous, I'll give you that. But he's a bum. He's just like Will Hager, and I don't need another one of those."

"Will Hager? Is that the longhaired guitarist you went out with back when you first started here?"

Amanda nodded.

"How can you think he and Hudson have anything in common?"

"They're both good-looking, they both could charm the skin off a snake—provided it was a female snake—and neither one of them has a paycheck."

"Yeah, but Will was leeching off you. Hudson hasn't tried to borrow money or raid your refrigerator or borrow your car, has he?"

"No, but I figure it's only a matter of time."

"So you're going to try and convict him before you've even given him a chance." Margie folded her arms over her voluminous bosom, challenging.

"He'll be leaving at the end of June," Amanda said a bit desperately, grasping at straws.

"All the more reason to stop wasting time." Margie took the check from Amanda's trembling hands. "I'll just deposit this. And I'm ordering you to take the rest of the day off. Go to the Clip 'n' Snip and get your hair done. Then go to Hudson Stack and grovel."

AMANDA DID AS ORDERED. It wouldn't hurt to be a lady of leisure for one day, in celebration of her big sale. She got a trim at Clip 'n' Snip, a two-chair salon on the square, and asked Reba, her stylist, to leave her hair loose. For this day, at least, she didn't have to look professional. Then she went home and, ignoring the huge tower of boxes still stacked in the living room, went up to her room and put on a short denim skirt and a halter top. If she was going to grovel, she would at least look good doing it.

Then she went next door and, her heart in her throat, knocked on the front door. She got no answer, but Hudson's car, a nondescript rental sedan, was parked in the driveway, so he couldn't have gone far.

Unless some other woman had taken him fishing.

Sagging with disappointment, she was about to return home when she saw a bicycle coming down the lane, looking a bit wobbly. Bicycles didn't often come this way, since her street was filled with potholes.

As the bicycle came closer, she realized it was Hudson, with Bethany on the back.

"Faster, Daddy. Go faster."

"Give your old man a break, kid. I haven't been on a bike in twenty years."

Amanda's heart lifted as a memory came into sharp focus. Her father had once driven her and Mick down to Galveston for a vacation, or what passed as one. They'd had to sleep in their car in a motel parking lot, and they'd made a game out of scavenging leftovers from tourists. But her father had found a twenty-dollar bill, and with it he'd rented a bicycle built for two. She'd ridden on the back, unable to reach the pedals, and Mick had sat in the wire basket on front. They'd had a blast going up and down Seawall Boulevard at least a dozen times, with Mick constantly laughing and begging their father to pedal faster.

Hudson might be a bum, but he loved his daughter, and that had to count for something.

She waved to them as they turned in the driveway, and Bethany jumped off the bike almost before it had stopped and ran to Amanda. She hugged her with unquestioning enthusiasm, apparently forgiving her for her several days' absence.

"See, Daddy, she's not giving us the runaround."

Hudson leaned the battered bike against a tree and gave Amanda a rueful grin. "I don't know where she gets this stuff."

"Well, I do, but I forgive you. Especially since you were right. How's your hand?"

He flexed the hand in question, which now had only an adhesive bandage across the palm. "Good as new. I already had the stitches out." He looked up at her with a reassuring smile, but the smile faded as he studied her for several heart-stopping seconds. "You look different."

"I took the afternoon off. Oh, you won't believe it! The most wonderful thing has happened. I sold the Clooney mansion!"

"Did you, now?"

"The commission will solve so many problems for me, at least in the short term. I don't know if you noticed, but I have another mouth to feed."

Looking surprised, he slid his gaze down to just below her waist, then back up again.

"Oh, no, not that. That's, um, not a worry anymore. I mean, Tonya moved in."

"And you just let her?" Hudson blurted out.

"She had nowhere else to go. She was living in her car. Can I help it if I'm a pushover?"

"You haven't been such a pushover with me."

"What's a pushover?" Bethany wanted to know.

"Let's go inside," Hudson said, still breathing hard. "I need something to drink. I hadn't realized I'd let myself get so out of shape."

Amanda eyed him critically. "You don't look out of shape to me."

"It's all flash and no substance, believe me. You wouldn't say that if you'd heard me huffing and puffing up that last hill."

He let them into the house. All the windows were open and a fresh breeze ruffled the faded curtains, keeping the heat of the day at bay for at least another hour or two. But the cabin had only one A/C window unit to cool it. Even with a breeze off the water, it was going to get hot here before the month was out.

"I don't think I could make it half a mile on a bike," Amanda said.

"Really? I hear exercise does wonders for your blood pressure. Have you measured it lately?"

"No, I haven't, and I don't want to talk about it." But Doc Hardison had been telling her to get more exercise.

"You could come riding with us. We go pretty slow."

"I don't have a bicycle."

"I got mine at a garage sale. Twenty bucks. We could find one for you."

"Hudson?" she asked as he poured a glass of Kool-Aid for Bethany and one for himself.

"Yes?"

"Why are you being so nice? I've been a complete jerk the last few days."

"I already told you, it's because you're my reflection. I know what's going through your head."

"Oh, really?" That would be embarrassing. Because at the moment, as she watched Hudson's Adam's apple bobbing up and down as he drank, her thoughts were pretty X-rated. She'd managed to block memories of their lovemaking while she was busy with work, but now that she was back at the scene of the crime, she could think of little else.

Hudson offered her a glass of Kool-Aid, but she declined. "You've been thinking," he said, "you don't have time to get involved with someone, and even if you did, I'm all wrong for you, anyway."

Amanda cast a nervous glance at Bethany, who was listening intently. Now she was waiting for Amanda's reply. Well, this wasn't something that should be discussed in front of a four-year-old.

Hudson refilled Bethany's cup and handed it back to her. "Why don't you go out on the patio and water our flowers?"

"Because I want to stay in here with you," Bethany answered.

"Okay, let me rephrase that. Bethany, go out on the patio and water our flowers, please. Amanda and I have grown-up matters to discuss."

Bethany pouted, but she did as asked.

Now Amanda was really nervous. Why had she brought this up in the first place? Hudson had seemed content to let her back into his life as if nothing had happened. Wouldn't it have been easier to just gloss over her recent bad behavior and go with the flow?

Too late now. She'd let the genie out of the bottle.

"What do you mean, I'm your reflection?" she asked. "It's the second time you've said that."

"Just that we're a lot alike."

Amanda was flabbergasted. She couldn't think of any two people who were less similar. "Would you care to elaborate?"

Hudson laughed. "You won't believe me, anyway." He drew her into his arms and kissed her soundly, sending her heart into overdrive and her hormones standing at attention.

"Congratulations on the big sale," he murmured. "You deserve it. Guess this'll show Mary Jo, huh?"

"Well, not exactly. It was her listing."

Hudson grew very still. "You're joking."

"No. I wish I was."

"The whole reason—I mean, I thought you were celebrating because you'd surged ahead of Mary Jo."

"I'm celebrating because I can pay some bills. And I've decided to let Mary Jo have June."

Hudson smiled. "Really? What's prompted such generosity?"

"Guilt," she answered without hesitation. "And my own selfishness. I've got the chance to spend two more weeks with this gorgeous hunk who lives next

door to me, you see. So why should I waste time bust-
ing my butt at work?''

"Now, that's what I like to hear." He pulled her
close again, lingering over the kiss.

"Mmm," she said, "you taste like cherry."

"You smell like vanilla."

"How many hours until Bethany's bedtime?"

HUDSON SPENT A FEW more delicious minutes discov-
ering new places on Amanda to kiss. Then it occurred
to him that he hadn't heard a peep out of Bethany for
some time.

Reluctantly he put a stop to his sensual assault. "I
have to go see what Bethany's up to. She's way too
quiet."

As Hudson and Amanda came outside, they found
Bethany on her stomach in a recently turned flower-
bed. Hudson's stomach swooped with momentary
panic, until he realized the child was nose-to-nose with
a turtle.

"Be very quiet," she cautioned them. "You'll scare
her."

"Her?" Hudson mouthed, looking at Amanda.

"I'm naming her Ashley."

"I thought we had a deal," Hudson said. "Shiny is
supposed to be your only pet."

"We made a deal about fish," Bethany pointed out.

Before the afternoon was up, "Ashley" had her
own little enclosure in the backyard, with a den made
from a cardboard box covered in leaves and branches.
She had her own private pond, made from a discarded

trash can lid, and a wide assortment of dietary selections.

Hudson convinced Amanda to stay for dinner. He'd been planning to pop a frozen pizza in the oven, but Amanda vetoed that idea. "Too much fat, too much salt."

"I thought you didn't care about your blood pressure."

"I do care. I just don't want to actually measure it." And she whipped up a chef's salad and potato soup. She even managed to convince Bethany that she didn't really hate salads.

Afterward, they went to Amanda's to watch *The Wizard of Oz* on video. She apologized profusely for the piles of boxes, some still packed, some empty. "Maybe it won't be so bad, having her here," Amanda said unconvincingly. "She and Mick are gone most of the time."

Hudson figured they showed up long enough to eat the groceries Amanda bought, change into the clean clothes Amanda washed, and then take off again, burning up the gas Amanda provided.

He knew it was none of his business, though.

Bethany was asleep before the flying-monkey attack. Hudson carried her home and somehow managed to climb up the ladder to the loft without falling or dropping his precious cargo. He covered her with just a sheet, opened the small window to chase away the stuffiness, then rejoined Amanda downstairs.

"Can you stay?" he asked, the three words charged with enough electricity to light up all of East Texas.

She flashed an embarrassed smile. "I was hoping

you'd ask. But can we be a bit more sensible about it this time?''

"Already taken care of.'' He'd bought a box of condoms at the drugstore. The clerk, a wizened little woman with blue hair, had given him the once-over when she'd seen the purchase, then her thin mouth had tensed into a hard line. Hudson wasn't familiar with how small-town grapevines worked, but he'd heard about them. He hoped he hadn't set Amanda up for embarrassment. Oh, but surely they weren't that backward, even in Cottonwood, Texas. "So you're not pregnant?''

"No, I'm not.''

Hudson knew he should feel good about that. But at least if he and Amanda had a baby, she couldn't waltz out of his life. They would have a connection. "We won't be so careless next time, I promise.''

Amanda took his hand and wound her fingers between his. "Pretty sure of yourself, huh?''

"Just optimistic. And I certainly don't want you flying out of here afterward, upset because you'd done something that you hadn't thought through a dozen times first.''

"Is that how you see me?''

"Yes. And I'm right.''

Amanda looked uncomfortable. "You are right. That's the scary part.''

"It's scary to let someone know you.'' He pulled her to him and held her close, stroking her silky hair. It *was* scary, letting anyone close. He'd never let Elaine be privy to his innermost feelings, his fears, his sense of loss when a patient died. She'd tried to open him up, but he'd shut her out. It wasn't the way of the Stack family, to let feelings show in untidy displays. Better to be stoic and suffer in silence.

As a cardiologist, he knew how damaging it could be to bottle up emotions until they ate away at you from the inside out. As a flawed human being with a lifetime of bad habits, however, it was much harder to put theory into practice.

By shutting Elaine out, he'd lost her—to a man whose emotions were so messy that he would sob out his sorrow and grief in public, and to his mistress's husband, of all people. Hudson didn't want to be like that. But neither did he ever want to take a woman's love for granted and withhold crucial parts of himself until he drove her away.

*Then why don't you tell her who you are?*

He would, he vowed to his conscience. Soon. But Amanda was special, and a little too concerned about money for him to take it lightly. If she was going to fall in love with him—and that was a big *if*—he wanted to make damn sure she fell in love with a poor maintenance worker, not a millionaire doctor.

# Chapter Nine

The second time they made love, Amanda was far more relaxed. Instead of merely being driven nearly insane with desire, she could revel in each small sensation. She could also spend more time and energy finding out what pleasured Hudson.

His body was like a new and mysterious land to be explored, tamed and conquered, and she left no square inch of the terrain undiscovered. She found out he had ticklish feet. And that a small spot just below his right hip could make his whole body go rigid with passion, if she flicked it with her tongue just right.

She couldn't get enough of his flat stomach, and the play of light over the rippling muscles there when he spoke or laughed or sighed. She was fascinated by the diamond of hair on his chest, which was soft rather than coarse, tickling rather than scratching her cheek when she rubbed up against it like a needy cat.

His arousal held its own fascination. She'd never really thought of a man's…equipment as beautiful before. But Hudson's was poetry in masculinity, silk over steel, pulsating warmth, as vibrantly alive as the man himself. She spent endless minutes stroking, exploring, listening for the minute changes in Hudson's breathing and the noises he made low in his throat that indicated she'd done something that pleased him. She filed away her experiences for future encounters. She wasn't sure how much she could learn and build on in less than three weeks, but she intended to find out.

When Hudson had had enough of her teasing, he handed her a foil packet. "I'll do it if you don't want to."

"Of course I want to." She made sheathing him into another bit of foreplay, drawing it out to such a degree that Hudson suddenly grabbed her and flipped her on to her back, pinning her to the mattress.

"You're going to regret getting me so worked up. I'll be in and out in two seconds."

She chuckled low in her throat. "Somehow I doubt that. But let's find out." She opened her legs and guided him to her entrance.

"Are you sure you're ready?" he asked, his brow furrowed with concern.

He was worried because their foreplay had been mainly focused on him this time, she realized. But his concerns were frivolous. "Believe me, I'm ready. I was ready hours ago when I watched you drinking that Kool-Aid."

"Really? I hadn't realized drinking was sexy."

"Just about anything you do is sexy, Hudson Stack." She grasped him by his rock-hard buttocks and guided him home. Oh, yeah, she was ready. He slid in easily all the way to the hilt, filling her so perfectly it brought her to tears.

Thankfully, Hudson didn't notice the moisture in

her eyes. His own eyes were scrunched closed as he battled for control of his body. It made her feel proud she could bring him to this state.

After a few moments his face relaxed and he started to move inside her. Now she was the one battling for control, willing the pleasure to last into eternity. She would have been happy if they could have stayed joined all night, rocking together and apart, together and apart.

She held herself in check for a little while longer, but then the effort became too much and she relaxed and let nature take its course. An earthquake started at her center, spreading out in shock wave after shock wave of tingling pleasure.

Hudson put his hand over her mouth, and she realized she must have cried out. Then he tensed and reached his own climax.

His eyes were clenched shut. She wished he would open them, wished they could gaze into each other's eyes, each other's souls, as they shared this wonderful, simultaneous climax. But he revealed nothing of his feelings in his face.

After a few moments he relaxed and slumped against her, though he was careful not to put all of his weight on her, shifting slightly to the side.

"Worth the wait, Amanda."

She threw her arms around his neck and kissed his cheek. It irritated her that she'd let her confused emotions keep her apart from Hudson all these days, when she could have been making love with him every night, sharing meals with him, delighting in Bethany's antics. It wasn't like her to waste opportunities.

Well, no more, she thought as she settled drowsily into Hudson's arms for the night. For the rest of the month, she was going to enjoy herself. Oh, she would put in her hours at work. But not fourteen hours a day. And she would take off at least one full day per week, during which she would not even check her voice mail.

For the rest of the month, so long as Hudson and Bethany wanted her around, she would see how the other half lived—the half that didn't have to work so damn hard.

HUDSON WAS AMAZED at the changes he saw in Amanda in the days that followed. Her alabaster complexion took on a honeyed glow from the kiss of the summer sun. She wore her hair loose, or sometimes piled into a tumble on top of her head, a far cry from the tight confines of her previous twist, anchored by dozens of pins.

Even her body language changed. She talked and moved more slowly, laughed more, and didn't seem compelled to be moving every second she was awake. She held her jaw differently.

And he was responsible, he thought with quiet pride. In his more egotistical moments, he believed he'd saved her from a future with a debilitating heart disease. He hadn't yet coaxed her into measuring her own blood pressure again, but he was pretty sure it would be lower.

His own was. Oh, it wasn't back to normal. But it was moving in the right direction, and more than a few points. He figured he could return to Boston as scheduled, and his health would be so markedly improved that George would reinstate him immediately, even if everything wasn't perfect.

For the first time, the idea of going back home didn't cheer him up. He'd thought his stint in the sticks, with no one but a four-year-old for company, would be a boring punishment to be endured. Instead he was having fun, a concept that was as foreign to him as it was to Amanda. He'd meant it when he said she was his reflection. They had so much more in common than she would ever know.

They rode bikes. Margie from Amanda's office had loaned her a clunker from her garage, and the three of them must have made quite a sight, poking around the streets of Cottonwood at a snail's pace. The local dentist, Allison Hardison, sometimes caught up with them and rode for a mile or two. But then she would surge ahead.

"She's a very serious cyclist," Amanda explained. "I'm sure our pace was boring her silly."

"We're getting faster," Hudson pointed out. And they were. That little hill on their street hardly bothered him anymore.

When they weren't riding bikes, they were fishing in Ed Hardison's boat or hiking a nature trail or having a picnic of baked chicken and potato salad made with fat-free mayonnaise. On one of their outings, they'd found another turtle, which Bethany named Bubba after a fisherman they'd met at the marina. They staged turtle races, offering grapes as an incentive.

In the afternoon, when it was very hot outside, they sometimes retreated to the air-conditioned coolness of

Amanda's house to play Monopoly or Chutes and Ladders or Battleship. And always, after Bethany was asleep, they would make passionate love.

Amanda was so changed, in fact, that Hudson started to worry that she'd gone too far. Her attention to her work was haphazard at best. She slept late, took long lunches, came home early. And she hardly mentioned her work at all.

So one day Hudson decided to question her about it. They'd taken Ed's boat to a sandy cove, cooked turkey dogs over a fire for lunch, then went swimming. It hadn't taken long for the food and sun and activity to wear Bethany out, so she was napping on a towel in the shade. Hudson and Amanda were resting their arms on opposite sides of an inner tube, bobbing on the gentle current and gazing at each other.

"What time do you have to be back at work?" he asked her casually.

"I have to meet some clients at the office at four, so I can float around here for at least another hour."

"Don't you have to prepare for them?"

She waved away his concern. "I can do a quick search right before they get there. They're looking for a house with a pool, though, and I already know we hardly have any listings that will qualify. So it's probably a bust." She closed her eyes and laid her cheek against her arm, taking a deep, contented breath.

The Amanda he'd first met wouldn't have settled for that. She would have searched for houses with big backyards and tried to convince her clients they should build a pool. She would have gotten brochures from swimming pool companies, and obtained a few estimates on different sizes of pools. She might have even talked the couple into buying lake property, so they wouldn't need a pool.

"Amanda, maybe it's none of my business, but you seem awfully casual about your work these days."

She cracked open one blue eye. "Yeah? What about it? I thought that was the idea."

"Well, it is, to a point. I'm just a little worried. Your career is so important to you, and I don't want you to damage your reputation by being *too* casual about it."

Now she opened both eyes. "Is that so?"

"I'm not meaning to offend you, Amanda. I'm just concerned."

"You're kidding, right?"

"Um, no. Why would you think that?"

"Just that I find it ironic that a man with no job sees fit to criticize the way I manage mine."

"My lack of employment isn't the issue here."

"Well, maybe it should be. I worry about you, too, you know. No visible means of support, a child to look after, and you haven't even talked about getting another job, much less actually looked for one."

Hudson felt his jaw tense. "I see. I guess my financial status *is* an issue."

"No, that's *not* the issue," she said hotly. "I don't care about money. I don't need some guy to buy me flowers and diamonds and take me out for steak dinners."

"Then why do you care if I'm unemployed?"

"Because…because I don't want to end up supporting you and Bethany, too," she blurted out. "I've spent my whole life taking care of people who couldn't provide for themselves, and I don't need it anymore.''

He was so surprised by her answer that he couldn't respond. He'd wanted Amanda to think he was an average guy—not a poverty-stricken potential leech.

''I've always taken care of myself and my family,'' he said when he could finally speak. ''Have I ever given any indication that I expect you to take over that job?''

''No,'' she admitted. ''You've obviously got at least some money, for groceries and such. But what happens when it runs out?''

He was on the verge of telling her it would never run out, even if he never worked another day in his life. His trust fund alone provided enough for a lavish lifestyle. And Bethany had her own trust, from her mother's family.

But now, more than ever, he needed to know where Amanda stood. Could she be just like all those other women he'd rejected, the ones who'd been looking for a free ride? He could reassure Amanda so easily, but he didn't want to. He wanted to see how far she would take this argument, and how much of a double standard existed in her mind.

''I solemnly swear I will never ask you to support me,'' he said. ''I'd live in the street before I would do that.''

''But I would never *allow* you to live in the street. I care about you, both of you, whether you want it or not.''

''That's ridiculous. Amanda, I won't end up on the

street. I have plans. I just prefer not to talk about them.'' Because they involved moving back to Boston, and he wasn't ready to deal with the issue of whether she could move with him. It was too soon for that.

''Think of the example you're setting for Bethany,'' she tried again. ''Do you want her to think life's just a big party, and no one has to work until they're forced to?''

''She doesn't think that,'' Hudson said, getting really ticked now. The most important aspect of this vacation was his relationship to Bethany. He'd never been this close to his daughter. To insinuate that he was doing her harm by taking time off from work and spending it with her—it was ridiculous.

''Children do learn by example,'' Amanda said quietly.

He sighed. ''Well, if you're so sure I'll end up as your charity case, maybe you'd better get back to work. Maybe you're setting a bad example for me!''

''It's different in my case.'' Her hands gripped the inner tube so tightly he worried her fingernails would pierce the rubber. ''I've given myself the rest of the month to take it easy and lower my blood pressure, and only because the Clooney mansion commission gave me some breathing space. But it's temporary, just until the end of the month. I haven't had a vacation in years—hell, I've never had a vacation, unless you count the weekend in Galveston when I had to sleep in my car and eat leftover pizza that was someone else's garbage. So don't talk to me about work habits.''

''I'd appreciate it if you'd return the favor,'' he said

quietly, most of the fight gone out of him. That comment about eating garbage pizza had really gotten to him. Apparently Amanda had once been poor—really poor. And what did he know about that? He'd never gone hungry in his life. Even with his hectic work schedule, he always managed to eat something, because he couldn't afford to be light-headed or shaky during surgery.

"Maybe we should get back," she said. "You're right, I'm neglecting my work. Just because I deserve some time off doesn't mean I should shortchange clients who depend on me." She dived under the inner tube and came up near shore.

Hudson paused a moment to watch her coming out of the lake like Venus, water running off her in sparkling rivulets, her hair hanging straight to the middle of her back, her skimpy bikini leaving little of her tanned, toned body to his imagination.

Shaking his head, he headed for shore, too. He should have kept his mouth shut, damn it. That would teach him to show concern.

THE NEXT DAY, Amanda buried herself in work out of pure guilt. Hudson was right, she *had* let things slide, and she might very well be doing damage to her reputation. As a real estate agent, her reputation was everything.

She ended up selling a house to the swimming-pool couple. She'd gone door to door in a newer subdivision in Mooreville, two towns away, where almost everyone had a swimming pool. Eventually she'd found someone who'd been thinking of selling. She'd put buyer and seller together, and everyone was happy.

"So, does this put me ahead of Mary Jo?" she asked Margie as they were going over the paperwork at Margie's desk.

"I thought you weren't going to worry about it this month."

"I'm not worried, just curious."

"Well, sorry to say, sweetie, but Mary Jo's leaving you in the dust."

"Really?"

"Emily's ahead of you, too, and even Hank is nipping at your heels."

"Oh, my God. What's Jerry going to think?"

"Honey, with the Clooney mansion, it's the company's best month in history. Jerry does not care."

Amanda stood, suddenly antsy, and paced the small reception area. "But I didn't even work for that sale. It fell in my lap! And I've been such a lazy bum—"

"Stop it. You needed some time off. And you seemed to be enjoying yourself. What happened?"

Amanda threw up her hands. "I don't know. Everything was going well, and then Hudson started questioning me about work and how I was being lazy—"

"Did he say that? Did he use that word?" Margie demanded. She clenched her plump fists, looking as if she wanted to take someone's head off.

"No, he didn't use that word. He said he was worried I'd relaxed *too* much. I should have just told him the reason I wasn't spending much time at work was because I wanted to spend every waking moment with him, and that I don't want him to leave at the end of the month."

"So what did you say instead?"

"I turned around and attacked his work ethic. I said he was setting a bad example for Bethany."

"Uh-oh. Something tells me he didn't like his fatherhood getting criticized."

"I don't know what I was thinking. He's a wonderful father. The best. In fact, he reminds me—" Amanda stopped, horrified at what she was about to say.

"Bingo," Margie said softly.

"Wait, that can't be true. My father was the town drunk. I've never even seen Hudson tip a beer."

"But that wasn't *all* your father was. You forget, I went to school with Danny Dewhurst. He was kind and generous, and when your mama was pregnant with you, I thought he was going to burst with pride. Now, it's a shame about his drinking—"

"And smoking. And gambling. And philandering."

"Okay, so he was weak. But he was loving."

"If he'd loved us, he'd have at least tried to take care of us, instead of making my mom do it all."

Margie pursed her mouth. "I guess it's hard to reconcile those two things—loving but irresponsible."

"It's impossible. He was selfish and weak and a real pain in the posterior."

"And you still miss him."

Amanda sighed. "Yeah. Guess I'm a sucker for lazy bums. Hudson included. I told myself I could go with it for this month only, because come July, Hudson and Bethany would be gone and I could get back to the real world. But things haven't worked out exactly as planned.''

''You think too much, you know that? Maybe Hudson shares some questionable traits with your father. But he also shares a few good ones, doesn't he?''

''Yes,'' Amanda admitted.

''You're not planning to marry the guy. So enjoy yourself.''

''But what if—''

Margie held up her hand like a traffic cop. ''I don't want to hear it. It's almost five o'clock. I'll finish this paperwork. You go find Hudson and patch things up. Don't let it go on and on like you did last time you got spooked.''

''I'll go home and fix dinner, but I've got an appointment at seven to do a CMA in Mooreville.''

''Well, you better call and cancel. Have you looked outside lately?''

Amanda looked out the front window. It was darker than it should have been. ''I haven't turned on the weather in days. Did something roll in?''

''We're under a severe thunderstorm watch, last I heard. So you better call and cancel,'' she repeated. ''You don't want your pretty car to get hail dings in it.''

Margie was right. On her way home, Amanda called her potential clients and rescheduled for tomorrow evening. Then she parked her car in the garage and dragged all of her potted plants on the patio against the house, where the roof overhang would protect them from hail.

The huge cumulus clouds billowing up in the southwest were so dense they were black on the bottom, but the sun illuminated their tops, so they resembled charred marshmallows. The wind had picked up, too, causing the trees in the woods behind her house to sway alarmingly. Amanda eyed some of the larger trees in her backyard with trepidation, and prayed the weather would spare them. It wasn't uncommon around here for a big storm to send a tree crashing right through someone's roof.

She peeked next door. Hudson's car was there, but she didn't see any lights inside the cabin. If he and Bethany were out biking or hiking, she hoped they weren't too far from home, because the skies were about to let loose. She could smell the ozone in the air.

Mick and Tonya weren't home, either, but at least they had a car. They could drive to shelter. She hoped they had enough sense to do so.

She turned on the Weather Channel, then dialed the number at the cabin, hoping to find that Hudson and Bethany were safe and she'd worried for nothing. But the phone rang and rang. She could only hope they weren't out on the water, though they probably would have taken the car to the marina if that was the case.

She watched the Weather Channel for a few minutes, hardly comforted by what she saw. Cottonwood had been upgraded to a tornado watch. She walked next door and rang the doorbell, just in case Hudson hadn't answered the phone for some reason. But they definitely weren't home. She peeked into the open garage and realized Hudson's bike was gone.

The first fat raindrops fell, and Amanda's worry

ratcheted up a notch. Surely Hudson would stop and take shelter. But what if they were out on those country roads that cut through the nearby National Forest? No farms or gas stations out there.

She decided she had to go look for them. She backed her car out of the garage, praying for no hail, and headed out Highway 17, a rinky-dink two-lane blacktop that wasn't bad for bicycling. As she passed the Red Dog Saloon, she searched for Mick's car, but she didn't see it.

That was one bit of reassuring news, she supposed.

She turned on the radio to the all-news channel out of Tyler. Though static punctuated the broadcast, she could still make it out, and the storm was the big story of the day. It was heading for Mooreville, and it was dropping buckets of rain. There'd been some unconfirmed sightings of twisters, but Amanda tried not to let that bother her too much. Any time there was a storm that involved roiling clouds, people thought they saw twisters.

On a hunch, she turned down a farm-to-market road they'd ridden on many times. Rain fell harder now. Amanda turned on her windshield wipers to high and scanned the road ahead of her. It was deserted. On either side, the cattle had bunched up to better withstand the driving rain.

Just when she was about to give up, she spotted a dot coming over a hill in the distance. As she got closer to it, she realized it was, indeed, Hudson and Bethany.

Her relief at finding them safe was short-lived. As she pulled to a stop and flashed her lights at them, just to make sure they didn't ride right past her, the radio announcer delivered some unpleasant news.

"We do have an official sighting of a tornado, which has touched down seven miles southwest of Mooreville in a sparsely populated area. The Weather Service has upgraded the entire Tri-County area to a tornado warning, which means you should take immediate shelter underground or—"

Amanda didn't wait to hear the rest of the warning. She'd lived in this part of the country her whole life, so she well knew what tornadoes could mean.

She popped her trunk lid and jumped out of the car just as Hudson's bicycle pulled up with her.

"Well, you're a sight for sore eyes," he said with a grin.

"We're all wet," Bethany announced unnecessarily.

Amanda lifted Bethany off the bicycle. "Get into the car, sweetie, and warm up." She opened the Lincoln's back door, and Bethany scrambled in.

"I don't mind riding in a nice summer rain," Hudson said as he unfastened his helmet, "but this is a little much. How'd you happen to find us?"

"I've been driving all over looking for you, that's how. There's a tornado on the ground, and it's headed this way."

# Chapter Ten

At news of the tornado, Hudson's movements became a bit more urgent. "Oh, hell." He jumped off the bike and wheeled it around to the trunk. "The bike's all muddy. Are you sure you don't mind?"

"Of course I don't mind." She grabbed one end of the bike and helped him heave it into her trunk. It fit, even without removing the front wheel.

"I've never seen such a huge trunk," he said.

She slammed it closed. "Never mind that. Just get in the car. We have to get to shelter."

They could have stopped at any number of places, but Amanda felt the best, safest location was her own house. Aside from the fact that it had a garage for her car, it was situated on the back side of a small hill that might offer some protection. And it had a basement, a real rarity in limestone-rich Texas. They were only a few minutes from the lake, and she figured they could make it to shelter in plenty of time.

Unfortunately, the hail started before they made it home. Marble-size pieces pelted Amanda's car, cracking sharply like gunfire with each impact.

Bethany screamed and scrambled over the front seat

to the dubious safety of her father's arms. "Don't let it get me, Daddy!"

"It's not going to hurt you, sweetheart. It's a loud noise." He wrapped his arms around her, and she buried her face in his neck. Amanda knew Bethany should be in the back, her seat belt securely fastened. But somehow she couldn't bring herself to object to the current arrangements. She was driving so slowly, anyway, she doubted they'd have an accident. They were in more danger of being hit by lightning.

"I'm glad we didn't have to ride through this," Hudson said, trying to lighten the mood.

"You could have been killed."

"Don't be melodramatic," Hudson said. "We're safe now."

Amanda just shook her head. "I don't know what kind of storms they have in Boston, but in Texas, you don't mess around with the weather."

"They say everything's bigger in Texas, even the hail," Hudson observed mildly.

As if on cue, the hail grew to the size of jawbreakers. Fortunately, Amanda's one-car garage was in sight. She pressed the button on the automatic opener. The door opened, revealing a maroon car already occupying the narrow space.

"Oh, great, Tonya's stolen my garage. My poor car!"

"Put it in my garage," Hudson offered. "I'll have to move some things—"

He really didn't get it. "No time. We need to take shelter. I have a basement." She cut the engine. The hail had let up for the moment. "Ready?"

They flung the car doors open and made a run for the front door. Since they were already soaked to the skin, they couldn't get much wetter, but the rain was so hard they almost had to swim to get to the door. Amanda quickly got the door open and they all dashed inside. But Bethany immediately darted back out again.

"My turtles. I have to save my turtles!"

Hudson tried to grab on to her, but she was too quick and she set off for the cabin next door. He was after her in a flash. "Bethany, come back here."

Whether the wind whipped Hudson's words away or Bethany chose to ignore them, Amanda didn't know, but the normally obedient little girl didn't stop. Hudson took off after her, and Amanda followed.

Hudson caught up with Bethany in a few strides and grabbed her.

"Daddy! The turtles!"

He handed Bethany to Amanda. "You go inside with Amanda. I'll get the turtles."

Amanda took a protesting Bethany inside just as the public defense sirens went off. That was a bad sign. It was pure insanity for Hudson to risk his life for a couple of turtles, who could probably take care of themselves just fine. But he would do it for Bethany.

Amanda set Bethany down just inside the front door, wondering if there was any point in trying to keep the rest of the house from getting muddy. Tonya met them with a couple of towels.

"Thanks," Amanda said, surprised at the courtesy. Tonya wasn't a bad person—she was just normally very self-absorbed.

Now she looked unusually pale and scared. "Thank goodness you're okay. You haven't seen Mick, have you?"

"No," Amanda replied, a frisson of alarm running up her spine. "I figured he was with you."

"He went out—wouldn't tell me where he was going."

"Tonya, wherever he is, I'm sure he took shelter, which is what we need to do."

The front door opened. Hudson stood there on the front porch, one turtle under his arm, another in his hand. The poor creatures were shut up tightly in their shells. "What do those sirens mean?"

"A tornado's been spotted in the area," Amanda said. "The basement's this way."

It wasn't much of a basement, just a small hollow carved out of the limestone bedrock. A trap door in the pantry led down a narrow flight of stairs. Amanda opened the door and flipped on a light.

The basement was full of boxes.

Tonya wrung her hands. "I wanted to straighten up so you wouldn't be so mad at us," she said miserably.

Hudson again stepped in to the rescue. He handed the turtles to Amanda. "Let me." In a matter of a minute or so, he'd cleared out enough space for the four of them to squeeze in. He left a couple of boxes for them to sit on. Then he drew Bethany onto his lap. Her crying had diminished to occasional sniffles.

"Now, this isn't so bad, is it?" he said to her, stroking her hair.

Bethany didn't answer. She inspected the new digs

with big, curious eyes, finally ending up staring at Tonya. "Who's that?"

Amanda realized Tonya and Bethany hadn't ever met. She made hasty introductions.

Tonya tried for a winning smile. "It's nice to meet you, Bethany." Then her hand went over her still-flat tummy and her eyes went dreamy. "I really can't wait until I have a child of my own."

"Are you gonna have a baby?" Bethany asked, entranced with the idea.

"Uh-huh. Around next Christmas."

"Will you let me hold it?"

"Of course. You can be my little helper. Would you like that?"

Bethany smiled, then looked at her father. "Can I, Daddy?"

Hudson looked uncomfortable. "I'm afraid we'll be back in Boston by the time Ms. Green has her baby."

"But we could come visit."

"Maybe we'll come visit, then," Hudson said. He looked over at Amanda. She held his gaze for a second or two, then looked away. She didn't want to think about the future, not yet.

Amanda remembered she had a transistor radio down here somewhere. She set the turtles on the floor—they weren't going anywhere—and rummaged around on a shelf until she found it, hidden behind a broken lampshade. She switched it on, surprised the batteries actually worked.

The static on the radio, though, was so bad they could only understand a few words now and then.

The wind outside blew harder. The walls actually

vibrated. Amanda prayed that her house would remain standing and that no one would be hurt.

The single light went out, plunging them into inky darkness. Bethany squealed.

"It's okay, sweetie." Amanda said. "The electricity always goes off in a storm."

"Is the tornado gonna get us?" Bethany asked tearfully.

"We're in a safe place," Amanda said, trying not to think about the tornadoes she remembered from her childhood. One had taken out the Baptist church in Mooreville, but that was the closest Cottonwood had ever come to a direct hit in her lifetime.

"I don't like the dark, either, Bethany," Tonya said in a shaky voice. "But we can be brave together, okay?"

"'Kay," Bethany said uncertainly.

Oddly, Amanda felt a new respect for Tonya. Amanda had spent so much of her energy resenting Tonya's intrusion into her life and focusing on her negative qualities, she hadn't bothered to think of Tonya as a whole person. Maybe Tonya wasn't perfect, but she apparently had some good traits, too, as well as some fears and insecurities and probably a crummy childhood she was trying to overcome.

The wind had grown to a roar, so loud it was hard to talk. In fact, it sounded like that proverbial freight train everyone mentioned in connection with tornadoes. The storm must have been going right over her house.

Amanda felt a hand reach over and take hers. She grabbed on to it for dear life, relishing the security

Hudson represented. Not that one man could fight off a tornado, but she felt better just having him near. She squeezed back.

With almost comic abruptness, the roar let up, and it got eerily quiet. The light came back on. Self-consciously, Amanda released Hudson's hand.

"Do you think it's over?" Tonya asked.

The radio was silent, now, except for the static. Amanda wondered if the storm had taken down the tower. "I guess we should peek outside and see if we still have a house."

Amanda climbed up the stairs and pushed the trap door open. There appeared to be a pantry still standing, at least.

She emerged into the kitchen. "Hey, we still have a roof." The others came out behind her. The relief was almost palpable.

Amanda did a quick inventory of the house. No broken windows, no apparent leaks. In the living room, the Weather Channel was still blaring.

"It looks like the worst has moved north of here," Tonya said.

Bethany, who had a traumatized turtle under each arm, gasped. "Shiny! I forgot Shiny." She looked up at Hudson. "Do you think he's okay?"

"I'm sure Shiny's fine," Hudson said. "As soon as the rain lets up, we'll go check on him, okay?"

Amanda stepped to the living room window, pulled back the curtain, and looked out. "Um, Hudson? I think there might be a small problem."

Hudson, Bethany and Tonya joined her at the window. They all just stared, speechless.

On the spot where the cabin had once stood, there was now nothing but a pile of firewood. Two large pine trees were uprooted and lying on their sides. One of them had crushed Hudson's car.

"Shiny," Bethany said, sounding dejected.

HUDSON COULDN'T BELIEVE how lucky he was. If Amanda hadn't come looking for them, they might be in the top of a tree right now. And if by some miracle they'd made it home to weather the storm, they'd have been crushed in the debris.

Tonya burst into tears. "I'm worried about Mick. He should have called by now!"

"The phone lines might be out," Amanda said, trying to soothe her. But the phone rang just then. Tonya pounced on it. "Hello, hello? Mick?" Her face sagged with disappointment. "Yeah, here she is." She handed the phone to Amanda.

"Amanda Dewhurst…yes, Margie, we're all fine. Are you at the office?" Amanda's face went white. "Oh, my God."

"What?" Tonya cried. "Is it Mick?"

"We'll do what we can." Amanda hung up the phone. "The tornado hit the shopping center behind the square. It flattened an entire city block, including the medical clinic. Margie said it's like a war zone."

"Injuries?" Hudson asked.

"Yes," Amanda said on a shaky breath.

"Where's the nearest hospital?"

"Tyler."

"But you have an ambulance service here, right? Some type of emergency response team set up?"

"I think so. But Margie said they needed help."

Hudson came to a decision. Although, really, there was no question what he had to do. "Tonya, will you stay here with Bethany?" He didn't want to expose his daughter to the trauma, if it was really bad, and she would only get in the way.

Tonya nodded. "Of course."

"Amanda and I will do what we can to help. And we'll try to find Mick." He turned to Amanda. "Get in the car and wait for me. I'll be right back." He quickly kissed Bethany, then sprinted out the front door and toward the pile of rubble that used to be his home.

Climbing over timbers and soggy plasterboard, overturned furniture and branches, he found the area that was once his bedroom. The mattress had been torn off the bed and was now in the driveway. But the heavy bed had remained in place. He reached underneath and found what he was looking for, grabbed it and then hurried back to Amanda's car.

He climbed in. "Let's roll."

"What's that?" she asked, glancing at the black leather satchel he'd recovered.

"First-aid kit."

"It looks like a doctor's bag."

"This bag belonged to my father." He was saved from further questions when Amanda was forced to stop the car. A gigantic limb blocked her path on the road. Hudson jumped out and dragged it out of the way, but with all the other debris in the street, it was slow going. Focused on her driving, Amanda apparently forgot about the black bag.

When they got closer to the center of town, a fallen tree stopped their progress. Amanda pulled her hail-pitted Lincoln to the side of the road. They got out and walked the rest of the way.

As they passed through the town square, they saw little damage except for a few pieces of trash and small branches blowing around. The ancient live oaks that shaded the square had come through unscathed. No windows were broken, although a few of the awnings were torn and flapping in the wind.

"Maybe Margie exaggerated."

But as they left the square and went around the barbecue restaurant, they saw a different picture, and it did look like a war zone. Cars were overturned. Telephone poles lay in the street like discarded matchsticks. And people were walking around, some bleeding, some merely wet and disheveled, and all looking as if they were in shock. The buildings on one side of the block seemed untouched; on the other side, nothing remained but a couple of brick walls, half-demolished. Billows of black smoke rose in the distance.

Hudson put his arm around Amanda's shoulders and gave her a quick kiss. "Be careful, okay?" Then he sprinted to the center of activity, where a man in a uniform with a bullhorn was trying to bring order to the chaos.

Hudson hadn't met the local law enforcement, but he'd seen sheriff's cars parked in front of the Miracle Café almost every time he'd come into town. The man talking appeared to be a sheriff's deputy.

Hudson interrupted him. "Excuse me. I'm a doctor. How can I help?"

The deputy turned to him. "Oh, man, can we use you. Luke Rheems." He shook Hudson's hand. "Some of the more seriously injured were taken into the hardware store. Unfortunately, we only have two doctors that live here. One is out of town and one is injured. The clinic's not usable."

"Don't you have an ambulance service here?"

"Our only ambulance is currently upside down. It was parked behind the clinic. We have a couple of paramedics, but they're with the volunteer fire department, and they're working on a gas fire, probably touched off by lightning. We've called for help, but no one's arrived yet. The bridge on Highway 60 is out."

"Where's the hardware store?"

Luke pointed across the street.

"Thanks." Hudson turned and loped across the street, entering the old-fashioned hardware store. Ordinarily he would have stopped to appreciate the funky little store with its wood floors, tin ceiling and merchandise crammed into every nook. Now, however, his gaze focused squarely on the seven people sprawled in the aisles, some on makeshift pallets, some on the bare wood. It looked like mostly cuts from flying glass, maybe a broken bone or two. A pretty woman in nurse's scrubs was bandaging the head of one man; several other people were doing their best to tend to wounds or offer a drink or reassurance to the others.

Hudson zeroed in on the nurse. "I'm a doctor," he said without preamble. "What's the situation?"

She seemed surprised at his sudden appearance, but grateful. "Not as bad as it looks right now, but these are the people who were able to walk away. I'm not sure what they'll find in the rubble. Two from our emergency response team are out of town, two are at a fire, and you're looking at the rest of it. I'm Sherry. This is Dr. Hardison." She nodded toward her patient.

The older man held out his left hand. His right hung at his side, his hand swollen and bleeding. "Ed Hardison. I'm afraid I won't be much use without both hands."

"Our clinic is a pile of rubble," Sherry continued, "and our one and only ambulance can't be driven. But I salvaged a few supplies." She nodded to a pile of sterile dressing, a box of rubber gloves, syringes, IV bores and a big bottle of alcohol.

"Why don't you start with that young man?" Ed pointed to a cowboy stretched out on the floor. "He was pinned under his truck. Says he's not hurt bad, but he's got a pretty good cut on his leg."

Margie was trying to stop the bleeding of the cowboy's thigh wound—and not having much luck.

"Here, let me," Hudson said, kneeling beside Margie. He pulled on a pair of rubber gloves, then quickly ripped away the denim of the man's jeans where it surrounded the cut.

"I didn't think it was that bad," the cowboy said. "I told Margie to tend to someone else, but—"

On closer examination, the cut didn't seem too bad. Hudson wasn't as worried about the cut as he was about the cowboy's chest. His breathing was labored, his jugular vein was distended and his trachea appeared deviated.

"Margie, I need you to apply pressure to that wound. Get some more sterile dressings and just pile them on top of each other and press." As he gave directions, he said, "What's your name?"

"Cal. Cal Chandler. I spent a year in vet school, so I know enough to know I'm messed up pretty good."

"You'll be okay. Breath deep for me, Cal."

One breath was all it took. "Sherry," he called out. "Cal here has a tension pneumothorax. I could use some help if you can spare it."

"I'll help." Hudson looked up to see Amanda kneeling across from him. "Just tell me what to do."

## Chapter Eleven

Amanda didn't ask questions. She just did whatever she could to help Hudson. She would have plenty of questions later, though.

"Put on some gloves and clean Cal's chest with alcohol, right here." Hudson indicated a spot on the left side of Cal's chest.

Cal jumped when she swabbed his skin. "Sorry, it's cold." But he didn't respond to her. His eyes seemed unfocused. He was losing consciousness, she realized.

Meanwhile, Hudson rummaged through the pile of supplies until he came up with a huge needle. He put on a fresh pair of gloves, then took a third glove and cut off one of the fingers. He inserted the needle into the finger and punctured the tip, then pulled the needle through until the finger rested on the end of the needle like a skirt.

"Sorry, Cal, this is going to smart."

Amanda gasped as Hudson punched the needle right into Cal's chest. Air that apparently had been trapped in the chest cavity rushed out of the IV needle with a hiss, causing the glove finger to flutter.

"Damn!" Cal shouted. Amanda did her best to keep

him still, throwing her weight against his shoulders. "What did you just do?" But then he smiled slightly. "Hey, I can breathe."

Hudson removed the needle, leaving a catheter in place. "Pack some bandages around that catheter to keep it stable," he instructed Amanda. "Margie, how you doing with the bleeding?"

"I think it's better."

"Keep the pressure going. He'll be fine." With that Hudson stood and peeled off his gloves.

"If you're finished there," Sherry said, "Mr. Buell here needs some attention. Here, I'll do Cal's dressing," she said to Amanda.

Mr. Buell, the owner of the hardware store, sat next to the cash register, gasping for breath. His complexion looked decidedly gray.

Hudson put on a fresh pair of gloves, then listened to the man's heart. "Mr. Buell?" he said. "You have a history of heart problems?"

"Yes, sir."

"You have medication?"

"Nitro. They're in my desk in the back, somewhere. Ain't had any trouble lately."

"I'll find it." Amanda ran to the back office, where she rummaged around in the desk until she found a small, black vial labeled "Nitroglycerin" that contained some tiny white pills. She ran back into the store and handed them to Hudson.

"Great, thanks." He removed one of the pills and put it under Mr. Buell's tongue. "Stay with him a few minutes," Hudson said to Amanda. "Yell at me if he gets worse."

More injuries were brought in—one man on a door being used as a makeshift stretcher, with a possible neck injury. "We didn't want to move him," one of the men carrying the stretcher said. "But he was right next to a wall that's fixin' to fall down. But we kept his head real steady."

"That's okay," Hudson said. "You did right." He further immobilized the man's head using products he found on the hardware store shelves—some Styrofoam packaging, a cutting board, duct tape.

"Has anyone seen my brother, Mick?" Amanda asked each new person that arrived. But no one had. She tried not to feel too anxious. Mick might be visiting a friend in a neighboring town or just hanging out somewhere that hadn't been touched by the tornado.

Hudson made his way around the hardware store, assessing injuries, reassuring patients, complimenting Sherry on her handiwork as she used Superglue to close up a cut.

Finally he got to one little boy who'd been sitting quietly in a corner, cradling an injured arm. He looked to be about eight or nine. Amanda knew she knew him, but couldn't place his name.

"Can I have a look at that arm?" Hudson asked him.

"It's broken," the boy said, sounding almost happy. "You're not going to fix it right here, are you?"

"You don't want me to fix it?"

"No! I want to go to the hospital and get X rays."

"Let me just look. I won't even touch it."

The boy reluctantly moved his good arm away from

the injured one. Amanda could see, even from a distance, that it was bent where it shouldn't be.

Hudson winced. "Oh, yeah, it's broken. Just hold it against your body and keep it still."

The boy grinned. "See, my sister Kristin's been to the hospital twice, and she got all kinds of presents. Now it's my turn." His smile quickly faded, though. "Is my Grandpa Ed okay? And Cal?"

Then Amanda realized the boy was a Hardison. Mentally she snapped her fingers in recognition. Sam, the rancher's son. He was growing up so fast.

"I think everyone's going to be fine," Hudson reassured him.

Finally Amanda heard sirens in the distance. Miraculously, no one had died, at least not that she'd heard about. Most folks had heeded the tornado warning and huddled under heavy furniture or inside interior rooms. The volunteers would probably be going through the rubble all night, though, just to make sure.

Paramedics descended on the hardware store, conferred with Hudson, Ed and Sherry, and one by one started loading up the injured, taking Cal first. Mr. Buell was looking better and breathing more easily, but Hudson insisted he go to a hospital.

"Have you heard of injuries anywhere else?" Amanda asked one of the paramedics.

"A couple of idiots out on the lake almost drowned," he answered. "But this was the only place I know of that got a direct hit."

Mick didn't like boats, so she could rule him out there. Somewhat reassured, she wondered how else she could help.

She felt a hand on her shoulder and turned to find Hudson. "I'm going to the clinic with Sherry to see what else we can salvage in the way of medical supplies. The Red Cross is setting up in the school gym, so we'll relocate there. Can you stay here for a few minutes and help direct people where to go?" Without waiting for an answer, he handed her a set of keys. "Close it up when everybody's out."

As Amanda looked into his brown eyes, so intelligent and compassionate, a host of confusing feelings welled up inside her, not the least of which was anger.

"You're a doctor," she said, feeling stupid.

His gaze slid away. "Yeah."

"If this town didn't need you so badly right now, I'd...I'd choke you with your own stethoscope!"

He looked at her. "I'm sorry. I had my reasons for keeping quiet about it."

She sighed. "We'll talk later. Go save some more lives, Dr. Stack. Sheesh," she added under her breath. "A doctor."

Amanda put it out of her mind as she and Margie straightened up the hardware store and told everyone who stopped in looking for friends and relatives to try the school gym. Finally Amanda made a sign to that effect and stuck it in the window, then locked up the store.

The police had cordoned off all the rubble, allowing only trained rescue workers to search. TV news crews were rolling in, but overall, things seemed much calmer than when Amanda had first arrived on the scene.

"What do you think?" Margie asked. "Should we

check out the gym and see what they need? Maybe we could go to my house and make sandwiches or something.''

Amanda resisted the idea of going to the gym, because she knew Hudson would be there. She wasn't ready to deal with that yet. ''I need to find Mick.''

''Maybe he's home by now. The phone at the office was still working last I checked.''

They walked to the office, stepping over debris or kicking it aside as they went. Tri-County Real Estate hadn't sustained any damage that Amanda could see. She picked up the phone, got a dial tone, and called home.

Tonya answered. ''Hello? Mick?''

''I'm sorry, Tonya,'' Amanda said, ''It's only me. I guess that means Mick hasn't made it home.''

''No!'' she wailed.

Amanda felt for her. ''I'm sure he's fine. All the injured people have been taken to the hospital, and he wasn't among them.''

''Why doesn't he call, then? Isn't he worried about me?''

''He may not be near a phone that works. A lot of lines are down. If you want something to do, you can come to the school gym. The Red Cross needs volunteers, I'm sure.''

''I'm staying right here until I hear from Mick. Anyway, I have to take care of Bethany.''

''Is she okay?''

''She's fine. We're coloring.'' Tonya's voice got all warm and fuzzy when talking about Bethany. Funny,

Amanda had been sure the girl didn't have a maternal bone in her body.

Margie and Amanda raided the office kitchenette. They had all kinds of food stashed there. "Wait," Amanda said, "I've got a whole fridge full of Slimfast in my office."

"Oh, real comfort food."

"Hey, it's nutritious."

Loaded with all they could carry, they walked the half mile or so to the Cottonwood High School, where several dozen people were milling around in the gym. Some Red Cross workers had arrived and were setting up coffee, snacks, cots and phones. Amanda's eyes immediately sought out and found Hudson. He and Sherry were already at work in a makeshift clinic. Hudson was examining a middle-aged woman's swollen eye, while Sherry was trying to calm a half-hysterical teenager.

Amanda and Margie took their food to the Red Cross workers, who gratefully accepted it. They went to work opening boxes that contained toiletries and assembling survival kits of soap and washcloth, toothbrush and toothpaste, a comb, bandages, aspirin and granola bars.

"So," Margie said casually as they worked side by side, "you didn't tell me your Hudson was a doctor."

"You know darn well I didn't know, or I would have said something."

Margie tried, and failed, to suppress a giggle. "A bum. You thought he was a bum. So why did he keep his identity a big secret?"

"I have no idea. He claims he had a reason. But I

can't imagine what reason would justify his lying to me all this time.''

"What did he tell you he did for a living?''

"Nothing. Oh, he said he 'fixed things.' He just didn't mention that the things he fixed were people.''

Margie laughed.

"It's not funny. I mean, what else is he lying about? Maybe his wife is alive and well and waiting for him back in Boston.''

"Are you talking about Dr. Stack?'' one of the Red Cross workers, a tall, thin redhead, asked.

"Yes,'' Amanda said. "You know him?''

"I know *of* him. I don't know what he's doing here, but it's lucky he showed up when he did.''

"So who is he?'' Margie asked.

"Heart surgeon. He saved the Boston mayor's life a few months ago with quintuple bypass surgery. I saw him interviewed on CNN. He's also a multi-millionaire, and he invested a large portion of his own personal fortune in developing a new kind of heart valve.'' She sighed. "He's even cuter in person.''

"The Stack valve,'' Amanda murmured. Holy cow.

"So if he's rich,'' Margie asked Amanda, "why did he rent the Skillman cabin?''

That was the sixty-four-thousand-dollar question.

Amanda's curiosity came to a screeching halt when a young man burst into the gymnasium. "We need some help. There's a car went off the bridge on 67 at Coombs Creek, and two people are stuck inside.''

The Red Cross workers, who Amanda supposed were used to this sort of thing, mobilized into action. But Amanda just froze. "Mick,'' she murmured.

"Oh, now, honey, you have no reason to believe that," Margie soothed.

"I know he's in trouble, or he would have called home." She abandoned her task and walked straight up to the young man who'd come in. "What kind of car was it?"

"A Honda, I think. Red."

The blood drained straight to Amanda's feet, and she swayed dizzily.

A strong pair of hands grabbed her by the shoulders and steadied her. "Easy, there." It was Hudson. She leaned against him gratefully, absorbing his warmth and strength. "How many people in the car?" he asked the man.

"Two. They're alive, but they can't get out, and the creek's still rising."

Amanda pulled herself together. "That's my brother's car. I should go, I should…" Should what? Jump in the creek and try to save Mick and whoever he was with?

"You should wait here, honey," Margie said, taking her hand. "It's raining again, and it's getting dark."

"I'm about done here so I'll take you," Hudson said. "They have some rain ponchos over there." He pointed to a table, where a woman stood guard over some yellow rainwear. "Get us a couple. They may need a doctor at the scene. Ambulances are having a hard time getting through on 67, and they can't fly a helicopter in with this weather."

Amanda shot him a look of pure gratitude. Though

it wasn't practical, maybe not even sensible, he understood her need to go to her brother.

She got the raincoats, Hudson made sure Sherry was set, and they hitched a ride with two county sheriff's deputies heading that way.

In the back seat, Hudson took Amanda's hand and squeezed it. "They didn't tell me when my wife was injured," he said. "I was only sixteen miles away, speaking at a conference, and they didn't want to interrupt me. She died before I could see her. I don't know if your brother's hurt, but you should be with him."

"Thank you." She paused, then added, "I know who you are, now. One of the volunteers told me. The Stack valve."

"Yeah, that's me," he said, almost bitterly.

"You're a famous doctor, a millionaire, yet you led me to believe you were an unemployed maintenance man on the verge of poverty."

"You assumed that on your own. I just didn't enlighten you."

"Why not?"

"Because I was sick of being a famous doctor, okay?"

"But you have an amazing gift, a talent shared by maybe one in a billion people. Why hide it?"

He looked at her, and she didn't understand the pain she saw behind his eyes. "Because I didn't want you to look at me the way you're looking at me right now."

"With admiration? With awe?"

"You're looking at me like I'm a list of accomplishments rather than a man."

She sighed. "Okay, how about this?" She pulled her anger up around her and gave him her best scowl. "You made a complete fool out of me. I was actually worried you might go hungry if I didn't show you how to fish. And when you got that fish hook in your hand—you got a case of the vapors and said you hated the sight of blood!"

"That was real. I hate the sight of blood when it's mine. There was no way I could have pulled that hook out of my own hand."

She narrowed her eyes at him.

"Okay, I played it up a little."

"And if you have money, why did you rent that dinky little cabin?"

He gave her a guilty smile. "Mostly because it was next door to you."

That stopped her. Which was a good thing, because they'd arrived at Coombs Creek, and she needed to focus her attention on her brother.

The creek was swollen higher than Amanda had ever seen it, the normally tranquil water rushing under the bridge like a white-water river. And there was Mick's car, sunk nose first into the creek's soft bottom. Only a portion of the roof and the rear of the car were still above water.

"Oh, my God." She charged up to a man with a bullhorn who seemed to be running things. "Why can't you just break a window and pull them out?"

"We're afraid the water will rush in and drown

them before we can get them out. The girl's uncon-
scious.''

The girl? What girl was Mick with?

''We're trying to tow the car out.''

A pickup truck with a winch was parked on the
muddy banks of the creek. Three men were attempting
to anchor the truck so it wouldn't slide, while two
more were ducking under the water, apparently trying
to fasten the tow line to the Honda's undercarriage.

Amanda chewed one of her sculptured nails clean
off while watching the proceedings. Every once in a
while she saw movement inside the car, which gave
her hope.

The truck's winch started up and the line grew taut.
It strained and groaned, but the submerged car didn't
budge. Men with shovels attempted to move some of
the mud from around the car, but their efforts were
hampered by the rushing water.

All at once the tow line snapped, whipping back
and lashing at one of the rescue workers in the water.
He lost his footing and was almost washed away himself.

''Okay, hold it, hold it,'' the man with the bullhorn
said. ''Break that back window. It's the only chance
we have now.''

Amanda realized Hudson had disappeared. She
looked around, half panicked, worried he'd somehow
ended up in the water and gotten washed away when
everyone's attention was focused elsewhere. Then she
spotted him. He'd put on a harness and was tying himself to a line anchored to the bridge.

''Hudson, what are you doing?'' she called out.

Losing Mick would be bad enough. Losing them both…didn't bear thinking about.

A Cottonwood deputy—a man she'd sold a house to a couple of years ago—slid his arm around her. "It's almost over," he said.

The sound of glass shattering rose above even the noise of the roaring creek. Amanda held her breath as water rushed into the car. Rescue workers, Hudson among them, gathered around the broken rear window. They pulled out the inert body of a young woman.

Amanda recognized her immediately. "Oh, my God, that's Willow."

"Willomena Marsden?" the deputy asked.

"Yeah. She and Mick dated in high school." The implications were staggering. *Oh, Mick, how could you?*

Moments later the workers pulled a sputtering Mick from the car. Amanda almost collapsed with relief. She sent up a prayer of gratitude, then made her way to the creek bank, where someone had put up a tarp as a temporary rain shelter. By the time she got there, Mick was under the shelter being wrapped in blankets.

"Excuse me," Amanda said, working her way through the knot of concerned people around Mick. "I'm his sister. Can I get through, please?" Finally she reached him and threw her arms around him. "Oh, Mick, are you okay? Are you hurt?"

"I'm fine, just a little cold," he said through chattering teeth. "How's Willow?"

Amanda didn't see Willow. She didn't see Hudson, either, but she imagined he was working on her.

"You might want to ask about your fiancée,"

Amanda said tartly as some well-meaning first-aid worker stuck a thermometer in Mick's mouth.

Mick immediately pulled it out again. He looked stricken. "She's okay, isn't she?"

Amanda felt guilty for worrying him. "Yes, she's fine. Just worried sick about you."

He looked down. "It's not what it looks like, sis. I wasn't messing around with Willow. I guess there's no hope Tonya won't hear about this."

"None at all."

"She's been a little cranky since she's been pregnant."

"Get used to it."

"I'm not bailing out on her. I know you think I'm a complete screwup, but not this time. I'm going to be a good husband, a good father, I swear it. I just needed to talk to someone."

"You could have talked to me."

"Yeah, right. I didn't need a lecture. I just wanted to spend a little time with someone who didn't expect me to be someone I'm not. You and Tonya, you both keep looking at me like you're waiting for me to pull a rabbit out of my hat."

Amanda squeezed his shoulders. "I guess I've been a little hard on you lately."

"Nothing I don't deserve, I guess. Hey, go find out about Willow, huh? She was hurt. She hit her head."

Amanda put the hood back up on her poncho and headed into the rain. One of the patrol cars was pulling out, lights flashing. She saw Hudson standing by the side of the road, arms folded, his poncho long gone. He was drenched to the bone.

She approached him, touched his arm. He jumped. "Oh. Sorry."

"Where's the girl?" she asked.

He pointed toward the departing squad car. "On her way to the hospital. She regained consciousness, but she's lost a good bit of blood."

"Shouldn't you have gone with her?"

"A couple of volunteer firemen are with her. They're paramedics. She'll be okay. How's Mick?"

"Probably suffering from hypothermia, but he seems okay. Speaking of hypothermia…" She nodded. "You look like you could use some hot coffee."

He nodded, but a few minutes later, back at the gym, he refused the coffee someone offered him. He stood alone, away from the fuss everyone was making over Mick as they found him some dry clothes and took his blood pressure and made him sit in front of a space heater.

"You okay?" she asked Hudson.

"Yeah."

"You helped save my brother's life. You didn't have to do that."

"You aren't going to make a big deal out of this, are you?"

"Shouldn't I?"

"Only if it's in private and we're both naked."

Amanda's mouth opened, but no words came out.

"I'm sorry. I'm tired, and that just slipped out."

"Then why don't you put on some dry clothes and sit down for a spell? The world can revolve for a few minutes without you."

"That's what I worry about, though. Sometimes it doesn't. It's like, if I'm not on my guard every second, someone could die."

## Chapter Twelve

Hudson knew he wasn't making a lot of sense to Amanda. But as he'd gone into doctor mode, smoothly setting priorities, assessing injuries, reassuring patients, then performing whatever medical treatment was needed, he'd felt he was right back where he'd been before he'd ever heard of Cottonwood, Texas.

Yet it was where he belonged, what he knew best. He wondered how on earth he'd stayed away from it for so long. The moment things were under control here, he intended to call George and demand he be reinstated at General, or he would find another position. He felt better just having made the decision.

Amanda tugged on his arm. "Come on, Dr. Almighty. You're going to put on some dry clothes and eat a sandwich. You'll be no good to anyone if you keel over."

Amanda. Oh, hell. What was he going to do about her? *Thanks for the fishing lessons and some great sex, see you later.*

He let Amanda find him some dry clothes. He donned the SMU Mustangs T-shirt and some sweatpants behind a screen, tossing his muddy clothes into a garbage bag. Then he found a hard, plastic chair and ate a tuna fish sandwich and some potato chips, washed down with a soft drink.

Amanda sat beside him the whole time to make sure he ate, and he couldn't meet her gaze. He was afraid she would see he was thinking about abandoning her.

"So who was the girl in the car with Mick?" Hudson asked, to make conversation.

"Willow Marsden, his old girlfriend. He claims they were just talking."

"Do you believe him?"

"I shouldn't, not with his recent track record. But maybe it's true. He might have needed a sympathetic ear. A wife, a kid, finding a job—it's a lot for a guy like Mick to handle all at once."

"He better hope Tonya's as sympathetic as you are."

Amanda started to reply when a too-pretty man in a starched shirt approached the table where they were sitting. "Dr. Stack?"

Hudson sat up straighter, anticipating another injury needing his attention. "Yes?"

A microphone magically appeared in the man's hand. That was when Hudson realized there was a TV camera rolling not five feet away.

"I'm Paul Peterson with Channel 7 in Tyler," the man said, suddenly switching to a deeper voice. "I understand you saved some lives here today."

*Oh, hell.* "I'm not doing interviews," he said tersely.

"But you are Dr. Hudson Stack from Boston, right?

Inventor of the Stack valve, performed quintuple by-pass surgery on Mayor—''

Hudson grabbed the man by his shirt collar. ''What part of 'I'm not doing interviews' did you not understand?''

''Okay, okay,'' the reporter said in a panicked voice. ''Chill out. We'll just go interview someone else, okay?''

''You do that.''

Hudson released the reporter, who shot him a dirty look before grabbing his cameraman and moving on to greener pastures. ''Damn leeches,'' he muttered.

Then he turned and saw Amanda staring at him, her mouth gaping. ''What?''

''You have to ask?'' she said when she found her voice. ''That was just about the rudest thing I've ever seen.''

''Have you ever had reporters camp out on your front porch? Hound you when you have ten minutes between surgeries and you just want to eat your bagel in peace? Call you at home in the middle of the night, so that you have to switch your number six times? Or, or how about the one who masqueraded as a nurse and somehow got into my O.R.?''

''They really did that?''

''They bugged my car. They put it in the newspaper when my mother went in for an MRI. Do you want me to go on?''

''No,'' she said, sagging. ''But Paul Peterson's a nice kid.''

''I don't want any publicity. I don't want my picture in the paper. I don't want to be famous.''

"If you play God, people are going to worship you."

"I don't play God. They just treat me like one. And it's damned annoying."

He thought he saw a glimmer of understanding in her blue eyes. "So that's why you're slumming in Cottonwood. To get away from the attention."

"I took a vacation," he corrected her.

She shook her head. "I don't get you at all. You were born with every blessing in the world—good looks, intelligence and plenty of money. You have a talent, a skill, for saving lives. And you have a bright and beautiful daughter who loves you. Just what the hell do you have to complain about?"

"I love being a doctor, and I love Bethany. I don't care about the rest of it, and I wish nobody else did, either."

"You just think you don't care about money, but try getting along without it," she said, more to herself than to him.

He saw something, then, that made him stop and think. It was in her face, in the tension of her shoulders, and the self-conscious way she swiped a strand of her silver-blond hair behind her ear. That was when he realized she might not be his reflection after all. They might both have an overactive work ethic, but he was beginning to suspect it was for very different reasons.

IT WAS MIDNIGHT before things calmed down enough that Hudson felt he could go home and get some sleep. Then he realized he didn't have a home to go to. He thought about Bethany for the first time in several hours. He missed her.

He would forever be grateful to George for forcing him to take this vacation. He'd gotten to know his daughter in a whole new way, and he would treasure the memories of their time together.

"Have you seen Amanda?" he asked Sherry, who was also preparing to go home. She was worried about her stepson, Sam, the kid with the broken arm. It seemed everybody in Cottonwood was related to everybody else one way or another.

"I sent Amanda home with Mick a while ago. She was beat."

And he was part of the reason, Hudson thought guiltily. He'd been a real jerk about the reporter. One afternoon of high-pressure medicine had undone all the de-stressing his fishing vacation had accomplished.

"Hey, Sherry, do me a favor. Take my blood pressure."

"Okay," she agreed, though she had a curious look on her face. She found her cuff, pushed up his sleeve, fitted the cuff onto his arm and pumped it up.

A few moments later she released the air in the cuff and looked at him, concern in her eyes. "One-forty-eight over ninety-seven."

That was what he'd been afraid of.

"You've been functioning on caffeine and adrenaline all day," she said. "Check it again tomorrow. Maybe it'll calm down."

"Maybe."

One of the other volunteers dropped him at Amanda's house. He felt a little awkward about crash-

ing there after their strange conversation earlier—and
that ill-thought-out comment he'd made about both of
them being naked. *Smooth line, Dr. Stack.* But his kid
was here, and it was too late to make other arrangements, and he was just too damn tired.

The front door was open, and a small lamp in the
living room had been left on. Bethany was tucked in
on the sofa. A cardboard box containing Ashley and
Bubba was right by the bed. Hell, he was surprised
she didn't have the damn turtles *in* the bed with her.
He thought guiltily about Shiny. There was no way
the poor fish survived in that disaster of a house.

He resisted the urge to wake Bethany up and just
hold her. But she needed her sleep. He tiptoed past
the sofa on his way to the bathroom, and she stirred.

"Daddy?"

Relieved, he turned back to the sofa, sat down next
to her and gathered her into his arms. "It's me. How
you doing?"

"Tonya and me colored pictures, and then we
painted the turtles." She pointed into the box. Ashley
and Bubba appeared to be decorated with nail polish
and stickers.

"Very nice. I missed you."

"I missed you, too. Mick says you saved his life."

"A lot of people worked very hard to save his life.
It wasn't just me." But Bethany's adoration filled
Hudson with warmth, and he realized he didn't mind
being Bethany's hero.

"Did you fix anybody's heart?"

"No, but I fixed a leg, and a neck, and lots of cuts
and bruises. And one cat." That had been a first, but

he hadn't been able to turn down the big-eyed girl who'd shoved the wet, trembling animal at him and begged him to fix its leg. So he'd splinted the leg using a couple of plastic knives and some surgical tape, then wrapped the cat in a towel and told her to keep it warm and still, and find a vet as soon as she could. He had no idea if the animal had survived its ordeal.

"You smell funny," Bethany said.

"I'm not surprised. I went swimming in a creek today." He unwound her arms from around his neck and gently laid her back down on her pillow. "You go back to sleep, now, okay? I'll see you in the morning."

"Where are you going to sleep?"

A very good question. "I'll find a spot somewhere." But there was only one place he really wanted to sleep, if she'd have him.

He took a quick shower to rid himself of the layer of mud that still clung to him, then wrapped a towel around his waist and headed for Amanda's room in the loft. If she wouldn't have him in her bed, at least maybe he could snag a pillow and blanket and stretch out on the landing.

He quietly opened the door, expecting to find it dark. Instead, the room was infused with the glow of several candles, burning on the nightstands and the dresser.

And then there was Amanda, wearing a virginal white gown and seated cross-legged, leaning against the center of her headboard.

She smiled at him shyly. "About time you made it home. The candles are starting to burn out."

"Either I'm reading everything wrong, or this is a…seduction?"

She nodded. "I felt bad about our argument. You were under a lot of stress, and the reporter was obnoxious, and just because you have money and privilege and talent doesn't mean your life is perfect. I had no right to make that judgment."

Hudson climbed on to the edge of the bed, almost afraid to go nearer, afraid he would touch Amanda and immediately lose himself in her.

"I overreacted. I was hopped up on adrenaline. I'll apologize to Peter Paulson—"

"Paul Peterson."

"Whatever. I'll send him a basket of fruit."

"This doesn't have to be a seduction," she said nervously. "I just didn't want to go to sleep with this between us. You're probably too tired…"

"The day I'm too tired to make love to you, you better order up a pine box." He stood and dropped the towel, leaving her in no question as to how much he wanted her.

"Oh, my," she said, blushing sweetly.

They pushed all the covers to the foot of the bed. It was a warm night that didn't demand blankets. They piled all of Amanda's pillows—she had six—up against the headboard. Then Hudson laid her down on the mountain of feather-soft pillows. He simply gazed at her for a few moments, at the way the candlelight glowed in her hair and on her ivory skin, and the expectant look on her face.

Her breath caught as he reached under the hem of her nightgown and skimmed his hands up her legs.

She shivered slightly, reminding him all the more of some pagan virgin sacrifice.

A sacrifice to the conquering hero.

He tried not to think about that as he pulled the nightgown up and off her body. She was naked underneath. Her rounded breasts, now paler than the rest of her with her newly acquired tan, seemed to beg for his touch. The rosy nipples puckered before he'd even made contact.

Following instinct, he blew a stream of warm breath on to one of her nipples. She squirmed, but he held her fast and blew on the other one.

"This was supposed to be my seduction," she said in a hoarse whisper. "What are you doing to me?"

"Playing." He kissed her stomach, then finger-combed the soft curls guarding her femininity.

She gasped at the sudden intimacy. "Oh, yes, there. Just right there, that feels so good."

Was it his imagination, or was Amanda unusually enthusiastic in her encouragement? No. No, no, no, he wasn't going there. Nothing had changed just because Amanda now knew he was a millionaire. She'd made love to him when she thought he was poor and unemployed. He had to remember that. And if their love-making seemed more intense tonight, well, they'd shared life-and-death experiences today. All that emotion was bound to seep into their sex.

Amanda parted her legs to give him better access, and he forgot all about doubts and motives, because he was sharing a bed with the most beautiful woman he'd ever seen, let alone touched, and that was plenty enough to fill his mind. She certainly couldn't fake the way her skin quivered wherever he touched her, or consciously create the heat and moisture that pooled where he caressed her between her legs. She couldn't fake those endearing little gasps of pleasure whenever he moved just so.

And when she peaked unexpectedly, well before he was ready for her to, it was a climax not even Meg Ryan could have faked.

He laughed low in his throat and gathered her against him while she trembled in the aftermath.

"That wasn't fair," she whispered.

"All's fair in love and war."

"Your clichés don't convince me. I was supposed to be seducing you."

"And why does it have to be that way, huh?"

"Because I…" She stopped herself. "You're right, it doesn't matter."

"Come on, what were you about to say?"

"Never mind, it was stupid."

He kissed her, long and hot, teasing her with the tip of his tongue, until she was gasping for breath. "Talk or I'll torture you."

"How?" she asked, sounding intrigued.

"I'll make love to you continuously until you break."

"Is that supposed to scare me?"

He kissed her again. "Come on, Amanda. What aren't you telling me?"

He couldn't be sure, but he thought her eyes were suspiciously shiny, and she seemed to be blinking a lot. "Oh, all right. I wanted tonight to be just perfect, because I wanted to remind you how good we are together.''

''Why would I forget?''

''Oh, you could forget. I saw it in your eyes today. When you were working on Cal Chandler's chest. It was, well, it was artistry, poetry even. I saw it in your face. And no matter what inconveniences you face because you're rich and famous, you'll go back to being a surgeon. It's what you live for, what feeds your soul.''

He couldn't exactly argue with her.

''It's silly to think I could compete with that, with medicine and poetry and saving lives, but I wanted to try. There, I told you it was stupid.''

''Oh, Amanda. Baby.'' He hugged her and kissed her forehead. ''You're comparing apples and oranges.''

''Yes, but your apples are in Boston, and your oranges in Cottonwood.''

Undeniably true. But he didn't have to make a choice between those two right now. He rolled over onto his back and pulled her with him. ''C'mon, Ms. Orange. Let's do this thing up right.'' He was hard as a two-by-four, and he'd never wanted a woman as intensely as he wanted to be inside this one. Not even Elaine—not even during the height of their romantic courtship, such as it was—had made him feel this way.

Amanda Dewhurst was the real thing.

He kissed her neck and the hollow of her throat, then teased behind her ear with his tongue. She was so responsive that in almost no time he had her hot and bothered again. But he'd also worked himself into an almost frenzy.

"Enough," she said in a desperate voice. Then, "Please…"

"If you're going to beg…"

"Now is no time to be proud. I'm begging, you rogue." She grabbed the plastic packet she'd thoughtfully placed under one of the pillows, but he took it from her and handled the task of protection himself. If he let her do it, he might not make it inside her.

With a low chuckle he rolled over again, pinning her to the mattress, but she was a more-than-willing captive. She parted her legs and invited him in—an insistent invitation, actually, as she wrapped her legs around him and wasn't about to let go.

*Forget slow and easy,* he thought, plunging into her sweet depths with a sigh of satisfaction. It seemed that no matter what his intentions, once he was joined with Amanda, their lovemaking moved into hyper drive. She was just too delicious not to gobble up.

Still, he managed to hold himself in check until she reached another climax. Then he experienced his own sweet release, and for a few seconds, at least, he was able to forget Boston and Janey and his mother and the hospital and George and Bethany, and all the other umpteen things pulling on him, and just live in the moment.

As he gradually came back to earth, he thought about that—living in the moment. All of the literature he'd ever read about stress emphasized living in the present moment, rather than stewing over the past or worrying about the future. But until his stay in Cottonwood, he'd never understood it.

Amanda got up just long enough to blow out the candles. He disposed of the condom, then joined her back in bed, feeling a sense of satisfaction that went bone deep. He was meant to be with this woman, just as he was meant to be a surgeon. He just had no idea how he could do both in one lifetime.

"Do you want me to tell you the whole story?" he asked. "Or it can wait until tomorrow, if you'd rather sleep."

She snuggled up against him. "No, I want to hear it now."

"Okay." He took a deep breath, and he told her everything—about his job and the hours he worked, the surgery that saved the mayor's life, the idiotic magazine article that had turned him into a celebrity, his dismal medical checkup, George's ultimatum, and finally, Bethany calling the chauffeur "Daddy."

"I'm afraid I wasn't a very good father," he admitted. "I thought being a good father meant providing for my daughter, making sure she got into the best preschool, seeing that she had the latest toys and the highest-quality clothes and state-of-the-art medical care. That was my father's role in *my* life."

"Oh, Hudson, you mustn't discount those things," she said passionately. "Those are all really important."

"Yeah, but what will my daughter remember about me when she's older? Will she remember that I wrote a twenty-thousand-dollar check to a private school? Or will she remember that I took her fishing?"

Amanda didn't answer.

"What do you remember about your father?"

She sighed. "I remember the fishing," she admitted grudgingly. "And hikes through the woods and flying kites. But I also remember going to bed hungry. And when I did eat—well, let's just say to this day I can't eat canned baked beans or boxed macaroni and cheese."

The words poured out of her. "And I remember wearing clothes to school that didn't fit or were ten years out of style. And I remember my mother coming home late at night, smelling like Pine Sol, her hands red and raw, and my father sitting on the screen porch drinking beer and not even noticing how unfair that was. And I remember sneaking out of an apartment building at night with just one suitcase, leaving all my stuff behind, and later the landlord sold our stuff in a yard sale to make the back rent we owed."

Hudson felt such a growing sense of horror, he wanted to tell her to stop, that he couldn't take any more. He'd known she'd grown up without the advantages he'd had, but he'd had no idea the depth of her poverty.

Now he truly understood her strong reaction to his seeming lack of concern over his unemployment.

Still, she continued. "I remember that when my mother died, she would have been buried in a potter's field if some of the nice people she worked for hadn't paid for a cemetery plot and a few flowers. And after she died, the money ran out in a hurry and we were homeless for about two months."

"Homeless?"

"As in, we lived in a shelter in Tyler. I dropped out of school and took over my mother's customers. I remember my father stealing money from me one time to buy beer and cigarettes. If I'd had a gun handy, I'd have shot him."

Hudson got the distinct impression this was not merely a figure of speech.

"Later, I remember getting phone calls early in the morning, telling me which street corner my father had passed out on, and would I please come collect him?"

He didn't have any idea what to say to her, so he just stroked her hair.

"I'm sorry I dumped all that on you," she said in a shaky voice.

"I asked. Anyway, I'm glad you did. It helps me understand you."

"Why I work so hard, you mean? Well, I don't intend to ever scrub toilets again, that's for sure."

He was on the verge of telling her she would never have to work another day in her life, if she didn't want to. That she would never have to eat beans out of a can or wear anything but the latest designer fashions or live anyplace that didn't come with a maid. She was afraid of being poor again, and he wanted to remove that fear from her life forever.

But there was one slight problem. He was still entangled, technically at least, with another woman. Before he even thought about offering Amanda anything, he had to get his own life straightened out. And that meant returning to Boston as soon as possible.

## Chapter Thirteen

The next morning Amanda crept out of bed before the sun was up, leaving Hudson to his sleep. She felt drained from last night's confession, but sort of relieved, too. Finally, all the secrets were out in the open.

As she showered, she thought about her father, something she usually avoided. She found that the memories didn't jab her with their usual pain. She'd been angry with Dan Dewhurst for a long, long time, but reviewing her life with him had made her see something that had eluded her before. Dan had been as much a victim of his alcoholism as she had been.

He'd certainly made some poor decisions, and he'd been weak. But he'd loved her and Mick and their mother. He'd tried, especially in the early days, to make them happy. Once, Amanda had asked her mother why she didn't leave him. And her mother had answered that she was still in love with the man he used to be, and the man she'd hoped he would become.

Feeling more peaceful than she had in years, Amanda dressed, then mixed up some blueberry pancakes for breakfast. She and her cobbled-together family were going to celebrate everyone making it through yesterday's disaster alive and well.

Bethany woke up first and "helped" her with the pancakes. Then, one by one, everyone else drifted in, drawn by the mouthwatering scent. Hudson wore a T-shirt that read Touch My Harley and Die.

He shrugged. "I don't have any clean clothes. Your brother lent me this." Amanda suspected her brother had deliberately picked out the most inflammatory slogan he could find, thinking it was funny.

None of them said much at the breakfast table. Everyone was still processing yesterday's events. They murmured pleasantries, and that was about it.

Surprisingly, it was Mick who started the ball rolling. "Amanda, do you know which hospital they took Willow to? I'd like to find out how she's doing."

Amanda looked sharply at Mick, surprised he would even mention Willow's name in front of Tonya, then looked at Tonya to gauge her reaction.

Tonya just smiled. "He told me the whole thing last night. I was so happy he was alive, I couldn't even work up a good hissy fit."

Amanda was relieved to hear that. She thought for sure Mick would have lied or made up some excuse, like he'd picked up Willow hitchhiking or something.

"They probably took her to Mother Frances," Amanda answered. "I'll call and check on her, if you like." She had the phone number memorized from when her father had spent time at the Tyler hospital.

"Thanks." And Mick surprised her even further by

clearing dishes from the table and carrying them to the sink. Maybe there was hope for him yet.

Amanda called the hospital. Though they wouldn't release much information to her, since she wasn't family, they were able to tell her that Willow's condition was listed as good. She relayed that information to Mick.

Amanda then checked her calendar. She called everyone she had pending appointments with and canceled, explaining about the tornado to anyone who wasn't aware. She would spend the next few days helping people who'd been left homeless find someplace to live. A disaster relief fund had been started, so if she earned any commissions from sales or rentals to tornado victims, she would donate them to the fund. She figured it wasn't fair to cash in on other people's misfortunes.

Hudson drained his orange juice, then set the glass down decisively. "I need to go next door and see what I can salvage."

"I'll help," Amanda immediately offered. "I have to go to the office, but not till later. I'll try to find another place for you to stay, if you like," she added casually. "Of course, you and Bethany are welcome to stay with me. The more the merrier. But I'll understand if you want to get your own place. My house isn't exactly a palace."

*Please,* she prayed, *please say you'll stay with me.*

"Don't worry about us," he said. "You've got enough on your plate."

So, what did that mean? Was he staying? Moving

out? Going back to Boston? She was too chicken to ask him.

She grabbed a couple of trash bags and they went to the pile of debris that was once Hudson's cabin to see what could be salvaged. Bethany had wanted to come with them, but Hudson had said no. "It might be dangerous, honey," he'd said, but Amanda suspected the real reason was that he didn't want her to find Shiny.

There wasn't much to salvage. Part of the kitchen was still standing, with dishes and pots and pans intact. But the Skillmans would probably want to salvage those, so she left them. They found Bethany's dresser, still filled with her cute little clothes, damp but undamaged. But the chest of drawers from Hudson's room had been demolished, his clothes blown to who-knew-where.

In what had once been the living room, a door lay on top of the upended sofa. The shelves where Shiny's aquarium had once stood were now a neat stack of lumber. Amanda lifted some plaster wallboard and shoved it aside, and was astounded by what she saw.

"Hudson, come look at this."

He came over and peered over her shoulder at Shiny's aquarium, on the ground, right side up, unbroken, and full of water. Filthy water, but Amanda was pretty sure she could see a fish in there, still swimming.

"I'll be damned," Hudson murmured. "Let's turn him loose in the lake and tell Bethany—"

"Hudson!"

"Oh, all right. But I am not taking this fish back to Boston with me."

"So you're going?"

He looked at her, silently pleading with her to understand. "I have to."

She quickly turned away so he wouldn't see her tears. "Well, come on, Shiny, let's get you some clean water." With Hudson's help she hoisted the aquarium, and they carried it back to her house, where Bethany greeted her pet with squeals of delight. Amanda wished she could share Bethany's good cheer. With Hudson's proclamation, a pall had settled on what had started out as an optimistic day.

Mick and Tonya left for the hospital to visit Willow. Hudson got on the phone and wrangled with the rental company about his wrecked car. Amanda, meanwhile, helped Bethany clean Shiny's tank and get him situated in his new home.

"Can we go fishing today?" Bethany asked hopefully.

"Not today, sweetie. Lots of people lost their houses in the storm, and I have to help them find new ones. Remember how I helped you and your dad find a house?" Such as it was.

She nodded. "People always need my daddy, too. He's the only one who can fix their hearts, so that's why he has to work so much."

He might fix other people's hearts, but he'd broken hers into a million pieces.

Maybe she and Hudson were more alike than Amanda wanted to admit. They did both feel that the world would spin off its axis if they didn't personally keep it where it belonged.

"Well, at least for today, your daddy's home with you. So enjoy your time with him." She kissed Bethany on the forehead, kissed Hudson on the mouth—a little longer than a standard goodbye kiss—and headed for the garage door.

The front doorbell stopped her. "I wonder who that could be?" she asked as she went to open the door.

An attractive older woman, not a hair out of place, stood on her porch, a polite smile pasted on her face. Slightly behind her stood a brunette woman closer to Amanda's own age, but tall and slender, with huge green eyes and a trendy haircut.

"Hello," the older woman said pleasantly. "I'm looking for Dr. Hudson Stack. I was told I might find him at the home of Miss Amanda Dewhurst. Would that be you?"

Before Amanda could answer, Hudson came up behind her. "Mother? What are you doing here?"

Then the younger woman's face lit with pleasure. "Oh, Hudson, I've been so worried about you!" She practically shoved Amanda aside and threw her arms around Hudson.

For a second or two, Amanda entertained the hope that this gorgeous woman, who could have graced the pages of any fashion magazine, was Hudson's sister. Then the woman kissed Hudson full on the mouth—a bit longer than your standard hello kiss—and gave Amanda a pretty good clue as to her relationship to Hudson.

She broke the kiss and turned to Amanda, looking

chagrined. "I'm sorry, I didn't even introduce myself. I'm Janey Sessions, Hudson's fiancée. I'm sure he's told you about me."

Amanda pasted on a smile. "Why of course. In fact, he just couldn't shut up about you. Every other word out of his mouth was 'Janey this' and 'Janey that.'"

Janey looked inordinately proud to hear this news. Hudson just stared at his shoes.

"We're so proud of how he stepped in here and just started saving lives right in the middle of a hardware store. It's so lucky for you people that Hudson was here."

"Yes, we were lucky," Amanda agreed. "Lucky that such a fine surgeon ended up in our backward little town." She opened the door wider and stood aside to admit her new guests, though she wanted more than anything to slam the door in their faces, shut out reality.

"We've really missed him in Boston," Janey said, obviously not catching on to the uncomfortable vibes. "I'm sure his patients have missed him, too. He's slated to be the youngest chief of cardiac surgery ever at Boston General, when his boss retires."

Amanda kicked a mud clod off the threshold and on to the porch. "How lucky for Boston General."

"Some women don't do well as doctors' wives. They can't stand the pressure and the crazy hours. They just don't understand that a doctor's first priority is his work. But I do. I think medicine is like…like a sacred calling, and I could never, ever interfere with that. If I have to spend most nights alone, well, I don't mind my own company." She cast adoring eyes up at

Hudson as she clung to his arm as if it were the last remaining life vest on the *Titanic*.

"Well," Amanda said briskly, "I hate to run when you've just arrived, but I have work to do. Make yourself at home—everyone else has. Bye-bye." She escaped before she did anything to embarrass herself, like rake her nails across Janey's flawless complexion.

It wasn't Janey she should be angry with, anyway. It was Hudson. He seemed to have left out a significant part of the story he'd told her last night. A fiancée—like that would be so hard to remember. She shook her head, amazed at how naive she'd been to believe *all* the secrets were out.

"GRANDMA JUDITH!" Bethany yelled, and ran up to Hudson's mother with every apparent intention of hugging her. Judith Stack leaned down and grasped Bethany's shoulders before she could complete the hug, air kissing her on each cheek instead.

"Bethany, darling, how are you? Oh, goodness, watch those sticky fingers on Grandma's silk jacket."

Three weeks ago, Bethany wouldn't have even attempted a hug, Hudson mused. She'd become much more free with her affection since they'd been living in Cottonwood.

"Come give Janey a kiss," Janey said, and Bethany went to her happily, like a puppy. At least Janey knew how to hug. She scooped Bethany up into her arms and gave his daughter a proper squeeze. "Have you been having fun on your vacation?" She set Bethany back on her feet.

"Uh-huh. We went fishing and caught Shiny, and I

have two turtles, Ashley and Bubba. Come see them.'' She grabbed Janey's hand. Janey flashed Hudson a look that begged him to rescue her, but he didn't, so she went gamely to meet Bethany's new pets.

"So what's really going on here?" Judith asked. "I was surprised you chose such a strange place to vacation, not to mention that you ran off without telling Janey. George and Arthur both knew exactly where you were, but they wouldn't tell me. Now I find you shacked up with some woman—"

"I'm not shacked up with her," Hudson said, his irritation rising. "My rental house was next door. A tornado demolished it." He guided Judith to a window, where she could get a good look at the debris that used to be his cabin. "Amanda was kind enough to offer me a place to stay last night, or we'd have been sleeping on the gymnasium floor."

"Oh, my God," Judith said. "I knew a tornado hit the town, but I hadn't realized you were actually a victim. Were you hurt?"

"No. How did you find me, anyway?"

"I saw you on the Channel 9 news. They said you saved some man from drowning."

Hudson's heart sank. He'd been hoping the publicity surrounding him would have died down by the time he returned home, but this would only fan the flames.

"I called Janey," Judith continued, "and we caught the first plane to Dallas and rented a car. Since you weren't returning our calls," she said with a sniff, "we decided it was our duty to check on you in person."

"Well, as you can see, we're fine."

"I'll be the judge of that." She looked pointedly at his T-shirt, then rolled her eyes.

Hudson's jaw tensed. He noticed it because he'd started out the day pretty relaxed. He wondered if he always had a tense jaw around his mother and decided that might be the case.

"Sit down, then," Hudson said, trying very hard to be pleasant. It was all he could do not to run out the door after Amanda. But he didn't have a car, unless he hijacked the huge rented Cadillac Judith and Janey had arrived in. Anyway, he thought it best to deal with the two women before he tried to explain things to Amanda. "Do you want some coffee?"

"What kind of coffee?" Judith asked as she eyeballed the sofa and two chairs in the living room, trying to decide which of them would be least distasteful.

"I don't know. The kind you buy at the grocery store and brew in a drip coffee maker."

"No, thanks."

"I'd love some," Janey said from the sofa, where she was gingerly holding one of Bethany's turtles. "I don't care what kind it is, so long as it has caffeine. We've been up all night."

Hudson was glad for something to do with his hands. He filled a mug with coffee, then realized he didn't know how Janey liked it. Hell of a thing to be almost engaged to a woman and not know how she likes her coffee.

Amanda liked hers black.

"Can you recommend a nice hotel in the area?" Judith asked.

"You're staying?" Hudson asked, trying not to sound too horrified.

"Hudson, dear, we're exhausted. Even if we wanted to go back right away, we have to get some rest first."

"There aren't any hotels in Cottonwood. There are a couple of small motels, but I imagine they're filled up with tornado victims and volunteer workers. Maybe even media." He shuddered at the thought. "Tyler probably has something decent, but that's forty-five minutes away."

"Forty-five minutes," Janey repeated as Hudson handed her the coffee. "Thanks. It's funny how people in Texas measure distance in drive minutes."

Hudson hadn't ever thought about it, but it was true.

"Everything is so strange here," Janey continued. "The accents just kill me. When we stopped and asked a man at the Red Cross shelter where to find you, he went into this long-winded explanation about how some woman named Wynona had 'carried' you home last night. It took me a few moments to realize he meant someone had given you a ride." She laughed daintily. "And he told us to be careful crossing the bridge over the 'crick' because those waters were 'swole up something fierce.'" She laughed again.

Hudson didn't bother to point out that her accent, which sounded a bit like Miss Hathaway's on *The Beverly Hillbillies,* was probably just as amusing to the Texans as theirs was to her.

"Really," Judith added. "I don't see how you stand it down here. George has his nerve, blackmailing you into this."

"I like it here," Bethany piped up. She was lying on the floor, letting the two turtles crawl over her.

"Bethany!" Judith scolded. "Get those disgusting turtles out of the living room. Then wash your hands and come sit in a chair like a lady."

"Oh, let her alone," Hudson said. "She's just a little kid. Let her act like one."

"This place is turning her into a savage!"

"Maybe," Hudson said. "But she's a happy savage."

"Okay, fine." Judith folded her hands tightly in her lap. "You've had your little vacation. You called George's bluff. He dared you to come here, issued some sort of ultimatum, right? But now you've made your point. It's time for you to return to Boston and set things right. George was your father's oldest and dearest friend, and if you don't patch up your quarrel with him, I'm afraid you'll do irreparable damage to your career."

Hudson realized then that George hadn't told Judith the real reason for his exile to Texas. At least he'd honored doctor-patient privilege.

"I'm here because I needed to relax. I had a bad medical checkup."

Judith and Janey both grew very still.

"How bad?" Janey asked.

"High blood pressure, high cholesterol, that sort of thing."

Judith visibly relaxed. "Well, if that's all. You can take a pill to fix those symptoms. I'm surprised George would be so high-handed."

It had surprised Hudson, too, until he'd started to

actually relax. Then he'd realized how truly stressed out he'd been. "Coming here was a good thing," he insisted now. "I needed some time away…from everything."

"You could have told me," Janey huffed. "I could have gotten some time off and come with you." Janey didn't exactly have a job, but she was on the board of several charitable organizations.

"Then I would have spent the whole time worrying whether you were having a good time," he countered, not wanting to hurt her feelings. But Janey was definitely one of the things he'd needed time away from.

Janey smiled. "That's very sweet."

Oh, if she only knew.

"I have a marvelous idea," Judith said. "Pack up your things, and we'll all drive back to Dallas. We can be there in time for a late lunch at the Mansion. We'll stay a couple of days, do some shopping, get massages. We'll do nothing but indulge ourselves. Then you can go back to Boston rested, relaxed, ready to work."

"That is a terrific idea," Janey enthused. "How about it, Bethany. Want to stay in a fancy hotel?"

Bethany sat up. "Can Amanda come with us?"

Janey looked at Hudson. She reminded him of a frightened deer. Did she suspect?

"Amanda has been very, very kind to us," Hudson said. "Bethany took a real liking to her." He needed to tell Janey the truth about Amanda. But later, in private.

"Well, of course she was kind to you," Judith said, a sneer in her voice. "For a struggling career girl like her, meeting a rich, handsome doctor is like pulling the arm on a slot machine. I hope she's not too disappointed when she loses her quarter.''

Hudson's jaw tightened even more. He wanted to scream at his mother that she'd gotten it all wrong. Amanda had been kind and loving long before she'd known he was a rich doctor. But objections from him would only elicit more questions, questions he didn't want to answer, at least not in front of his mother.

He needed some quiet time with Janey, so he could gently break the news that they weren't getting married after all. Not that he'd ever proposed in the first place.

''I can't just up and leave,'' he said decisively. ''I have some loose ends to tie up here. Why don't you two drive to Tyler, get a room, get some rest. Call me later and we'll make plans for dinner.''

''Will you at least turn on your cell?''

''Cell phones weren't working, last time I checked. But you can call here.''

''Hudson, I don't think I can drive another foot,'' Janey said. ''I was practically falling asleep at the wheel.''

''All right, then, I'll drive you.'' Anything to get them out of town and away from Amanda, until he'd had a chance to explain things to her.

Hudson found them two rooms at a Marriott Suites in Tyler. It wasn't quite the four-star accommodations the two women were accustomed to, but they deemed it acceptable for one night. Then he appropriated their car and drove straight to Tri-County Real Estate, where he found a man on the roof replacing lost shingles. Later he learned the man was Jerry, Tri-County's mysterious owner and Margie's husband.

Margie was inside. She arched her thin, penciled eyebrows at him. "If you're looking for Amanda, she's out showing property. But I'd be careful if I were you. She has a dangerous gleam in her eye this morning."

"I guess she told you."

"That your occupation and your financial status weren't the only things you were less than forthcoming about? Uh-huh." She looked at Bethany and smiled. "Bethany, sweetie, I have a giant tub of Tinker-Toys around here somewhere. Interested?"

Bethany nodded. Margie bent below the counter and reappeared shortly with the promised treat. She led Bethany into Amanda's office and spread the toys out on the carpet for her. "What are you going to build for me?"

"Mmm, a turtle."

"A turtle sounds wonderful. Can you stay by yourself in Amanda's office for a few minutes while your daddy and I talk?"

For the first time in his life, Hudson wished Bethany would pitch a screaming tantrum so he wouldn't have to be alone with Margie. He suspected their conversation wasn't going to be pleasant. But Bethany merely nodded and went to work examining the familiar toys.

Margie closed the door and folded her arms. "I am so furious with you I could just spit. Jerry and I couldn't have any kids. But if we had, we'd have wanted one just like Amanda. Now, Amanda has been through some tough times. And she definitely has issues. But I thought maybe you'd be the one to sort of round her out. I thought she was crazy if she let you get away, and I'm the one that convinced her to give you another chance.''

''Now I really wish I hadn't.''

''It's not as bad as all that—''

''A fiancée? A fiancée isn't bad?''

''We're not really engaged. Janey overstated our relationship.''

''Oh? And just what is your relationship?''

''Is that any of your business?''

''It damn sure is. I don't know what they do in Boston, but around here we look out after our own. Amanda doesn't have any parents to protect her, so that's my job. I've done a poor job of it so far. I can't believe I let you snow me. The rest of the world might think you're a great hero, but to me you're a big zero.''

''I was only trying to protect my privacy,'' he said. ''I had no idea I was going to come down here and…and fall in love.''

Margie's scowl immediately melted. ''Did you say love?''

He shook his finger at her. ''Don't you say a word. I haven't told her yet, and I have some things to work out before I do. But I have to talk to her. Where is she?''

Margie looked at her watch. ''She was taking some people to the Chestnut Arms Apartments on Sixteenth Street. Then she was going to the gym to see if anyone needed anything. That's probably where you'll catch her. I'll watch Bethany, if you want me to.''

''That'd be great.'' He gave Margie a big hug and kissed her on the cheek. She turned bright pink.

''Well, now.''

Hudson poked his head into Amanda's office, told Bethany he'd be back in a few minutes, then headed out to find his love.

## Chapter Fourteen

Amanda was in the middle of making a list of supplies the Red Cross needed at the shelter. If she couldn't get someone to donate what was needed, she would buy it. Because she knew almost everyone in town, she was uniquely suited to know who had what and might be willing to part with it.

"Antibacterial hand soap," one of the volunteers said.

Amanda wrote it down. Mike Slidell over at the garage bought that stuff by the carton. She could probably snag at least a couple of jugs from him.

She heard her name and looked up to see Hudson headed her way in that ridiculous T-shirt. Oh, hell, this wasn't the time or the place. She wasn't ready to hear his excuses about why he hadn't mentioned his impending marriage.

"Not now," she said before he could say anything. "I have to go to Grubbs Food Mart. Clem Grubbs said he had a whole carton of toilet paper that got squashed by a forklift, and he's willing to donate it." She kept babbling, not wanting Hudson to get a word in edgewise. Otherwise, she might just start listening to him.

And if she started listening, she was a goner, because he had this way of making everything sound reasonable. "Then I have to stop by Triple Z Barbecue—"

"I thought it was Triple G."

"Oh, right." She smacked her forehead. "They keep changing owners. It started out Triple D when the Dardens owned it, then it changed to Z when the Zetmeirs bought it. Now the Gaynors own it, and it's G. I guess that's as much of the sign as they can afford to change." Babbling, babbling.

Hudson followed her to her car. The sun was shining brightly, with only the hint of a breeze. Hard to believe the skies had been so black and the winds so wild only yesterday.

"Anyway," she blathered on, "Rich Gaynor is donating a ton of sliced-beef sandwiches for the relief workers, and—what are you doing?" she demanded as he opened her passenger door.

"Going with you. You'll need help carrying."

"You can't go with me. I can't deal with you right now!"

He climbed into her car as if he hadn't heard her. Exasperated, she slid behind the wheel.

"We have to talk now," he said. "I might not have time later."

"Because you're going back to Boston to marry Janey. If you want my blessing, you aren't getting it." She jerked the Lincoln into gear and backed out of her parking space, tires spinning.

"I *am* going back."

"You already told me that, this morning. Goodbye, have a nice trip."

"The work I did yesterday reminded me of how much I miss working as a doctor. Saving people's lives is what I was put on this earth to do. I can't give it up."

"That is just so noble. Excuse me while I roll down the window and—"

"But I'm not marrying Janey," he said, interrupting her feigned gagging.

That stopped her.

"She overstated our relationship. We're not engaged. If we've talked about marriage, it's only been in the most general terms."

"Janey's terms were pretty specific this morning," Amanda said, knowing she shouldn't even get into a discussion with him. "And you didn't exactly jump to correct her."

"Janey is sweet. I didn't want to hurt her or humiliate her there in front of you and my mother. Yes, we were dating. And maybe there was some expectation, even on my part, that we'd someday get married. But that was before I met you."

Amanda pulled into a parking space at Grubbs and cut the engine. Suddenly she was very interested in what Hudson had to say.

"Janey will make some doctor a very good wife," he continued. "But not this doctor. You see, I've fallen in love with a scrappy little blond real estate agent. She's not on the board of any big charities, but she runs around picking up toilet paper and barbecue lunches for people in need. And she saves pet fish and turtles from terrible fates. And she doesn't play tennis at the club, but she casts a mean fishing rod and does exciting things with a purple flake wiggler. And she befriended a little girl who needed a woman's influence. And she takes care of a brother who usually doesn't deserve it, but she does it anyway because she knows the meaning of unconditional love, and that is so, so rare.''

Suddenly Amanda couldn't catch her breath. This wasn't really happening…was it?

"So even though this isn't the most romantic location, and I'm wearing a Touch My Harley and Die T-shirt, and we're in the parking lot of Grubbs Food Mart getting ready to pick up toilet paper, I have to do this now. Will you marry me? Come to Boston with me, be my wife, be Bethany's mother? You would never want for another thing as long as you live. You wouldn't have to work at all if you didn't want to.''

Amanda chanced a look at him. He wasn't smiling. This wasn't a sick joke. He was serious.

Marry Hudson? In a heartbeat. She almost blurted out a yes. But then her mind wrapped itself around the word *heartbeat,* which made her think of blood pressure and cholesterol and stress. So instead of saying yes, she opened her car door.

"Come with me."

Hudson followed. "Did I miss something? Are you ignoring my proposal?''

"No, I just can't answer it yet." She took his hand and led him past the entrance to the grocery store and on to the drugstore. She made a beeline for the blood pressure machine. "Sit down. Stick your arm in that cuff.''

He started to comply, then halted. "Wait a minute. What does this have to do with marrying me?"

"I want to know what your blood pressure is."

"It's low. Okay, it's not low, but it's almost normal. I've been checking it at home."

"So show me."

"There's no way it'll be normal now. I just proposed marriage! What's your point here? If you're trying to torture me in retaliation for Janey—"

"Of course I'm not trying to torture you. The point I was trying to graphically illustrate is that just talking about moving back to Boston and resuming your old life probably sent your blood pressure skyrocketing. Yes, your work is exciting and you love it—who wouldn't? But the stress of that life is going to kill you.

"Unlike Janey, I would not make a good doctor's wife, at least not that kind of doctor. Bethany and I would not be happy spending every evening without you while you play God at the hospital."

"Play God? That's a bit harsh." She realized he didn't look quite as adoring and besotted as he had a couple of minutes ago. Well, hell, someone had to inject a dose of reality here.

"My selfish needs aside," she went on, "I won't sit by and watch you work yourself into an early grave."

"Then what do you want? You certainly don't want an irresponsible bum. If I'm to avoid that, I have to work. Anyway, you're one to talk about overwork."

"Move." She pulled him up from the blood pressure machine and took his place, sticking her arm in the cuff. She hit the button, and the cuff inflated and tightened around her arm.

*Please, be low,* she prayed. She'd been checking her blood pressure whenever she was near either of Cottonwood's two drugstores. As she'd cut down her work hours and slowed down the frenzied pace of her life, the numbers had come down.

The machine beeped and the verdict was in: one-twenty-nine over ninety-one. Not perfect, but a vast improvement over what it had been a couple of weeks ago.

"How did you do that?" Hudson wanted to know.

"I fell in love," she answered without the least hesitation. "And I started living in the moment, because the moment was all I had. I do love you, Hudson. But if I moved back to Boston with you and married you and nodded politely while you returned to a lifestyle that made you sick, I might as well be lacing your coffee with arsenic."

"Things would be different," he said. "I've learned my lesson. I know how to fish. I've spent time with my daughter."

"And how much fishing do you think you'd get done in Boston? For that matter, how much time would you spend with Bethany? It's not a one-time shot in the arm, this vacation. It's a wake-up call."

"I'll make time for my family."

"You think you will, now. But when you're faced with saving some guy's life or going to your daughter's soccer game, which do you think you'll choose?"

That stopped him.

"You can't be Boston's preeminent heart surgeon on a part-time basis. You just can't."

"Then what do you suggest? Should I become a part-time fry cook at McDonald's?"

She did have an idea. He could stay here. Ed Hardison was ready to retire, and Cottonwood would need another doctor. Hudson could still do surgeries at Mother Frances or any of a number of hospitals in the area. But he could get off that fast-track Boston treadmill. Forget about being chief of cardiac surgery.

She didn't have the nerve to ask him. If she wasn't willing to uproot her life to merge it with his, why would he want to do the reverse? He had much more to lose than she did.

"You have to do what you have to do," she said finally. "And so do I."

"You're turning me down?"

She called herself ten kinds of idiot, felt her heart squeeze so hard she was afraid Hudson would have to perform surgery on her right here in the drugstore.

She had a chance at something big here. Real love, the kind that comes along once in a lifetime. And security most people could only dream of. But she wouldn't stand by and watch Hudson kill himself. "Yes."

HUDSON JUST TURNED and walked out of the drugstore. He couldn't believe it. He'd had senators' daughters and supermodels propose marriage to him. He was Boston's most eligible bachelor. Yet he couldn't snag one feisty little real estate agent from Cottonwood, Texas?

He walked the few blocks back to where he'd parked his car. Just what the hell was he going to do now? Marrying Janey was out of the question. Now that he knew what it felt like to truly love and be loved, he realized his relationship with Janey had been laughably shallow. His marriage to Elaine had been more of a business arrangement than a love match. No wonder she'd looked elsewhere for emotional fulfillment. The grief he'd felt for her death had been more like guilt, for neglecting her so thoroughly, always thinking there would be time later to work on his home life.

Why hadn't he learned his lesson then? There wasn't always a tomorrow. The last time he'd gone fishing with Amanda, it hadn't occurred to him it might be the last time. Would he have done anything differently? Had he savored each moment? How about when they'd made love last night?

He walked into Tri-County Realty to pick up Bethany. Margie looked at him expectantly.

"Don't ask," he said. "If you want to dissect a marriage proposal gone bad, you'll have to do it with Amanda."

"What? She turned you down?"

"Yes, as a matter of fact." He opened the door to Amanda's office and found Bethany at Amanda's desk with all of the knickknacks lined up like little soldiers.

"Just look at those cobwebs," she was saying to the pencil sharpener, shaking her finger at it. "If those aren't gone by the time I get home from the spa, you're fired." She turned her attention to a stapler. "And Bridget, the eggs this morning were too runny.

Tell Cook she'll have to do better or I'll fire her. And then I'll fire you, and, well, I guess I'll just fire everybody.'' She swept all the knickknacks aside. ''Lots of people need jobs. I can replace you.''

Hudson groaned.

Bethany looked up, startled. ''Oh, hi, Daddy.''

''Are you playing Grandma Judith?''

''Grandma Ruth. She says the servants are no good anymore.''

Grandma Judith, Grandma Ruth. They were pretty much peas in a pod. Though he loved them both and he realized they were products of their upbringing, they were both snobs to the hilt. He knew they were both trying to bring up Bethany like a proper young lady, tutoring her to become a debutante and then the wife of a doctor, lawyer or CEO, maybe even a congressman.

Neither of them would encourage Bethany to become a marine biologist. Yet she spent a lot of time with one or the other of them. They'd both stepped in after Elaine's death and taken over his daughter's care, and he'd let them, because he had important work to do.

Yes, saving lives was important, but so was raising the next generation. The time he'd spent with Bethany this summer had been some of the most important in his life. But had he really learned anything? Or was he just going to resume his former life exactly as it had been before? Once he was back in Boston, would he have the guts to make changes where it counted— in his everyday life? Or would he stand by passively

and let his mother turn Bethany into a mirror image
of herself—or Janey?

"WELL, I NEVER would have guessed that Tyler,
Texas, would have such a nice restaurant," Janey said
as she put her napkin in her lap. After giving her and
Judith sufficient time to nap and recover from their
trip, Hudson had returned to the motel and asked Janey
to dinner. He needed privacy to break the news to her.
Judith had agreed to watch Bethany swim in the motel
pool, though she'd wrinkled her nose at the idea of
her granddaughter frolicking in such a public facility.

Now Hudson and Janey were at Bremond's Steak
House, which he'd heard served the best steaks in all
of East Texas.

"I'd like the petite filet," Janey said to the waitress.
"Rare. And if it's not still mooing when it gets here,
I'll send it back, so make sure the chef understands
rare, okay?"

"Yes, ma'am. And for you, sir?"

Jeez. Had he actually told Amanda that Janey was
sweet? "I'll have the baked chicken breast, please."

Janey raised her eyebrows. "You're not ordering
your usual half a cow on a plate?"

"I'm a heart surgeon. I should eat the way I tell my
patients to eat. I'd like to live long enough to enjoy
my retirement."

She waved her hand dismissively. "That's decades
away." She took a sip of her Bordeaux, then ran the
tip of her finger around the rim of the glass. "So, I
bet you're sick to death of this place. Why George

made you come here is a complete mystery. Why not Aruba? Or St. Croix?''

"It's not a bad place," Hudson argued.

"What in the world is there to do?"

"Lots of things. Fishing, bike riding, hiking through the woods. Turtle races," he said with a grin.

Janey laughed. She thought he was kidding.

"Freda and Calvin have been asking after you," Janey said, abruptly changing the subject. "They're having a fifth-anniversary party next week at Le Fleur's. I told them we'd come, depending on your schedule, of course. But I figured you could at least pop in for a nightcap."

"Actually, I won't be able to make it."

"Why not? You *are* coming back with Judith and me, aren't you? I mean, a tornado destroyed your house. Surely George doesn't expect you to stay here now."

"That's not the issue. Janey…I'm not going to marry you." He winced at the harshness of what he'd just said, but he didn't know how else to break it to her.

"Excuse me?"

"You're a really great girl, but I don't love you."

For a few awful moments she just stared at him, blinking owlishly, as if she couldn't quite get him into focus. Then she laughed, the sound harsh and brittle. "Oh…my…God. You're not actually telling me you believe in something as silly as love, are you? Love is for peasants. Love is for people who don't have anything else. For people who watch *Oprah* and go on *Jerry Springer.* Why else would so many poor people agree to marry so many other poor people?''

''Janey, that's…a repulsive attitude.''

''Oh, lighten up. Maybe there is such a thing as love. But it doesn't last. It burns out like a road flare. There are much better ways to determine whom you should marry. We've talked about this!''

''Like what?''

''Don't glare at me like that. It's not money. I have plenty of that. I'm talking about compatibility. We come from the same culture. We went to the same schools. Our families vacation at the same places. We understand each other.''

Hudson wasn't at all sure Janey understood the first thing about him.

''If not me, who?'' she demanded. ''Have you been seeing someone else?''

As long as he was being honest about his feelings, he might as well tell her the whole truth. ''Yes. I'm sorry, Janey. It just happened. But I really didn't know you considered us engaged.''

''Who?'' she demanded. ''Oh, God, it's not Buffy Winters, is it? She is such an airhead.''

''No, it's not Buffy.''

''Michelle Thurston? Kimberly Flagg? Who?''

''Amanda.''

Janey frowned. ''I don't know any Amandas.''

''Yes, you do. You met her this morning.''

''Oh. I don't remember….'' Then realization dawned. ''That woman? That fake bleached blonde? You're seeing *her?*''

''In the first place, she's a real blonde.'' Hudson

gripped his water glass so hard he was sure it would break. "In the second place, yes, I'm seeing her. I'm in love with her."

He hadn't actually said those words to Amanda. Maybe it would make a difference if he told her.

Janey laughed again, a little desperately. "You cannot be serious."

"I am. Maybe I'd better take you back to the motel."

"No, no, I think we need to explore this further." She seemed both amused and furious, which Hudson thought was a dangerous combination. Maybe he shouldn't have told her this news in such a public place.

He motioned for the waitress. "We have to go. Can we get our check, please?"

"I want my steak," Janey said, baring her teeth.

He slumped back into his chair. "Okay, fine. Bring the food."

The waitress nodded. "Yes, sir."

"So," Janey continued. "What are you going to do, marry her? God, if you're going to marry a gold digger, at least pick one who knows how to dress and talk and carry herself."

"Yes, I intend to marry her. She refused my first proposal, but I haven't given up."

"Refused? Why? Didn't she think the prenup was fair enough?"

"Janey, I really had no idea you were so cruel, or I wouldn't have wasted so much time dating you."

"Hudson. You've gone off the deep end, here. Now, I don't know what kind of hold this woman has on you, but I'm just trying to wake you up to reality. You bring that woman to Boston and try to make her fit in there and it'll be a disaster. Your family will be horrified. And Ruth—what would she say?''

Hudson had to admit he hadn't thought of what his former mother-in-law would have to say. His own mother was a snob, but Ruth Hanover elevated snobbery to an art form. Amanda would face a certain amount of resentment from his friends, family and associates, who would assume, as Janey had, that Amanda was after his money, pure and simple.

''Maybe she wouldn't be all that happy in Boston,'' he admitted, thinking aloud.

''So your alternative is to live here, and excuse me while I laugh, ha-ha.''

''You don't think I could live here?''

''Oh, puh-leeze. Picture this. You work at some backwater hospital where they don't sterilize their needles. You get up in the morning and drop Bethany off at school—*public* school, because I doubt there's a decent private school within two hundred miles. Then you go to your job, where you work on an endless stream of Bubbas and Lula Mays who've spent their lives clogging their arteries by eating everything fried in lard. For lunch you eat a tuna fish sandwich little Amanda-Lou made for you that morning. Then you go home to your trailer park, where your wifey has fried up chitterlings and hog jowls for dinner.''

Hudson just sat back and let Janey rattle on.

She was just getting warmed up. ''For entertainment you tip a few Budweisers at the Red Dog Saloon— God help me, there is such a place, I saw it with my own eyes. Or on a really special occasion you might go to a chili cook-off or—no, a tractor pull! Where you sit behind some fat guy in overalls and no shirt who hasn't bathed in a week. You drive a pickup truck and buy your clothes at the Wal-Mart. That sounds like a real delightful life, all right.''

Hudson looked down at the khakis and thick silk shirt he wore. Since the tornado had blown all his clothes away, he'd had to make a few emergency purchases this afternoon. ''These clothes aren't so bad. They came from Wal-Mart.''

Janey looked as if she might be ill. ''Oh, please tell me you're joking.''

''No.'' The funny thing was, the life Janey had described didn't sound all that bad. Of course, he'd live in a nice house instead of a trailer park, and his wife would fix stir-fry or veggie burgers instead of chitterlings—and sometimes he would do the cooking. And he was pretty sure they sterilized needles at Mother Frances. But taking his daughter to school, coming home in the evening, enjoying the local night life— that all sounded like fun.

Why hadn't he seen the obvious answer before?

Amanda was right. If he returned to Boston and resumed his old job, he would find it impossible to work shorter hours. He would fall right back into the high-stress lifestyle that would eventually be his downfall.

But if he lived here, he could still work as a doctor—just not twenty hours a day. And he could pull Amanda back from her own workaholic tendencies, remind her of what's important. He could forget being chief of cardiac surgery, and worrying about whether he drove the right car or attended the right club. He could be that average guy, the average dad he'd pretended to be when he'd first come to Cottonwood.

Their dinners arrived, and Janey dug into her steak wholeheartedly. "I might as well get something worthwhile out of this evening," she said. "I see I've only delighted you with my description of your future life."

"It's not my future life yet," he reminded her. "She said no."

"If she's not a complete moron, she'll change her mind." And that was the last they spoke all evening.

Hudson drove Janey back to the motel, then went to his mother's room. He knocked softly, figuring Bethany might be asleep. But when Judith let him in, he heard the shower.

"I was just rinsing the chlorine out of Bethany's hair," Judith said, stepping back toward the bathroom. "Where's Janey?"

Hudson stepped inside the room, leaving the door ajar. "In her room. Not speaking to me."

"What did you do to her?"

"I broke up with her, told her I was in love with someone else and that I'm planning to relocate in Cottonwood and marry Amanda."

Judith froze, turned and gasped at him, her mouth working but no words coming out. She reminded him of Shiny.

The motel room door opened wider and Janey stepped inside, her packed bags gripped in both hands. "Pack your things, Judith. We're going back to Boston. There's no point in wasting another minute on your idiot son. He's completely lost his mind.'' She stomped off.

Judith looked sad. ''You're serious about this?''

''I love Amanda, and you'll love her, too, once you get to know her. And Bethany...Bethany is just crazy about her.''

''Yes, Bethany's talked of little else. Much as I love Janey, I'm not sure she'd have made a very good mother.''

''Then you're okay with it?''

Judith sighed. ''I'm not an ogre. I just want what's best for you and Bethany. If living in Texas with Amanda makes you and Bethany happy—and I confess, I've never seen either of you quite so happy—I won't stand in the way.''

Hudson threw his arms around his mother and gave her a bear hug. Flustered at first, she finally hugged him back. He wasn't crazy, as Janey thought. He'd finally figured everything out.

## Chapter Fifteen

Cottonwood seemed to be getting back to normal. Those whose houses had been damaged had either done quick repairs and moved back in or found some other place to live, so the Red Cross was closing up shop. A city crew had cleaned the streets and sidewalks of branches and other debris, and bulldozers were making rapid progress on the collapsed shopping center.

But Amanda felt she would never be normal again. She'd gone in to the office to catch up on the work she'd neglected yesterday, but she was just going through the motions, counting the hours until she could go home and fall apart.

Not that she hadn't already. When Hudson and Bethany hadn't returned home last night, she'd been forced to confront the fact that it was over, really over, for her and Hudson. She'd cried herself to sleep like she hadn't done since her mother died, so that this morning she had scratchy eyes and stuffy sinuses and overall a poor attitude.

The office was unusually peaceful. Amanda would have preferred a crisis, a deadline, anything to take her mind off her questionable decision to turn down Hudson's marriage proposal.

On her third trip to the coffeepot, she found Margie in the kitchenette, staring at her curiously.

"What?"

"You have to ask?" Margie said. "I've tried to be polite and respect your privacy, but that doesn't come naturally to me. So *what happened?*"

"How do you know anything happened?"

"Because I told Hudson where to find you. Did he do it? Did he really ask you to marry him?"

Amanda nodded. "I turned him down."

"You what?" Margie put a hand to Amanda's forehead. "No sign of fever, but something must have made you delirious."

"I can't marry him. He has a fiancée. He's been lying to me about everything. I can't stand it when people lie to me. My father did it, Will Hager did it, Mick does it, and now I find out Hudson's no better."

"Oh, now, sweetie, you know Hudson is nothing like your father or Mick or that lousy guitarist. If he lied, it was probably to protect himself, not to hurt you. Anyway, he's come clean about everything now, hasn't he?"

"Only because he was forced to. And what if there's more? Maybe he's got a string of illegitimate children and a host of STDs. Anyway, I can't move to Boston and be a blue-blood doctor's wife. It's ludicrous. His mother hated me on sight, and his fiancée—she looks like a model!"

"But he chose you over her, so why do you care? I can't believe you would let a bunch of snobby Boston biddies dictate who you can marry or anything else."

"It's not that. You know I'd spit in Judith Stack's eye if she tried anything with me. You want to know the real reason I turned him down?"

"Of course I do! Give!"

"I'm afraid. I'm afraid he'll die."

"What? Hudson Stack is just about the most healthy specimen of the human male I've ever seen."

"But you're wrong. He has high cholesterol and high blood pressure and all kinds of stress-related illnesses. He has every intention of working himself into an early grave, and I'm not going to sit around and watch that."

"Now if that ain't the pot calling the kettle black...."

"But I'm getting better. I've learned. I've changed. No more working seven days a week, sixteen hours a day. I don't want to die young. I want to be there for my children and my grandchildren."

"But how are you ever going to have any of those if you don't marry Hudson?" Margie asked, apparently not quite getting the dilemma. "Amanda, honey, people die. Everyone dies someday. You can't live your life being afraid of it. You could marry the healthiest man in the world, and tomorrow he could get hit by a bus."

"Now that's a cheerful thought."

"It's true. Besides, maybe with you at his side, he'll get healthier. He'll be motivated, because he'll want to be there for your children and grandchildren, too."

Their conversation was cut short when the front doorbell chimed ferociously. Amanda's heart lifted for half a second as she wondered if it might be Hudson. Then Mary Jo slammed into the kitchenette, dropped her briefcase and made a grab for the coffee pot.

Margie and Amanda exchanged a glance. Amanda had never seen Mary Jo less than perfectly composed to the point of smugness.

"Something wrong?" Margie asked gently.

"The house on Crawford fell through. The title search was a joke—those people don't even own the house. The grandmother owns it, and she's not selling." Mary Jo turned a malevolent eye on Amanda. "So you'll be keeping your trophy another month."

The trophy? Amanda hadn't even thought about it lately. She didn't know what the totals were, but she'd been pretty sure Mary Jo was light-years ahead of her.

Mary Jo took her mug of coffee and her briefcase and swept out of the kitchenette.

"Am I really ahead of her?" Amanda asked.

"I don't know. Let's go check."

They returned to the front desk, where Margie accessed an accounting program on the computer.

"Sales price on the Crawford house was $152,000. If we subtract that from Mary Jo's total…you're ahead by a grand total of twenty-two bucks."

Amanda studied her list of sales and rentals for the month. "I know. Subtract out the last week's rent from the Skillman cabin."

Margie looked at her as if she was crazy.

"The cabin's gone. Hudson can't live there. We'll have to refund that part of his rent. That puts Mary Jo ahead of me."

"You've completely lost it."

"Just do it. I'm going to take the trophy and put it on Mary Jo's desk."

"But there's still a few days left of June."

"So what? Anyway, I don't think I'll be here to sell anything."

Margie's eyes sparkled with mischief. "Going to Boston, perhaps?"

"You've made me think, that's for sure." Amanda strolled into her own office, picked up the silly little trophy, and headed for Mary Jo's office. She tapped lightly on the door.

"Come in," Mary Jo said suspiciously. She looked as if she'd been crying.

Amanda entered and set the trophy on Mary Jo's desk.

Mary Jo looked at the trophy, then at Amanda. "What's that for? I don't want your charity."

"I have to refund one of my rentals. And I'm going out of town, so the trophy's yours, fair and square. Besides, you deserve it. You've worked your butt off this month."

"You mean it? I really beat you?"

"Yes. And you know, you sound just like I did the first time I beat Emily."

"I do?"

"It's not that attractive. In fact, I'm coming to believe the whole competition thing is counterproductive. Jerry started it as a joke, but then it got to be this intensely serious thing. If we all cooperated more, instead of competing, I bet everybody could sell more."

"Who sprinkled nice-nice fairy dust on you?"

Amanda had thought Mary Jo might benefit from what she'd learned. But maybe it was something Mary Jo had to learn for herself. "You're right, dumb idea. Enjoy your trophy while you can. It'll be back on my desk next month." If she wasn't in Boston.

Amanda got another nice surprise when she got home. The house was immaculate and Tonya was cooking dinner.

"Wow, this place looks great!" Amanda said.

Tonya looked uncertain. "You don't mind?"

"Mind?" Was the girl insane?

"It's just that my mother and I always fought about cleaning and cooking. She criticized the way I cleaned, and she wouldn't even let me in the kitchen. She said there was only room for one queen bee, and if I wanted to keep a house, I should get one of my own. So if you don't want me to cook—"

"No. No, no, no, no, I'd *love* it if you'd cook sometimes. And believe me, I have no complaints about the housework."

"Mick says you're particular."

"How would he know? He's never cleaned anything in his life."

"He has now. I made him do the vacuuming and dusting. And right now he's working. It's just a temp job with a construction crew working on the storm damage, but it'll buy a few groceries."

Amanda gave Tonya an impulsive hug. "You might just be the best thing that ever happened to my brother."

"Oh, and you have a phone message from Hudson. I saved it on the answering machine."

Amanda pounced on the machine before Tonya even finished her sentence. And there was Hudson's voice, pouring out of the machine. "I called because I have to return your key and we need to say goodbye." She wanted to wrap herself in that voice, drown in it. Oh, God, she loved him, she really, really did. And he was leaving, and she'd screwed everything up.

"How many times are you gonna play it?" Tonya asked, expertly flipping burgers on the grill. "He'll be here in five minutes."

"What?" Amanda played the message one more time and actually listened to the words this time, all of them.

"We'll be at your place around five-thirty. If you're not home yet, we'll wait."

"Oh, *shoot!*" She needed a shower. She had to put on better clothes. And she had to figure out how she was going to tell him she'd come off her high horse and she wanted to marry him after all. But the doorbell rang, and she ran to answer it.

"You don't know anything about playing hard to get, do you?" Tonya called after her.

She flung the door open. Hudson stood there, looking taller and more gorgeous than ever, with Bethany clinging to his back like a monkey. They stared awkwardly at each other a few moments. Amanda's mind was suddenly blank with panic.

Hudson spoke up first. "Come for a drive?" He pulled her out on the porch, where she could see the shiny blue pickup truck parked in her driveway.

"Is that what the rental company gave you as a replacement?"

"No, silly. That's my truck."

"Since when do you own a truck?"

"Since this afternoon. Just come for a drive."

"O-okay. No, wait. Tonya was fixing dinner."

"It'll keep," Tonya said from the doorway, spatula in hand. "Go."

Feeling a little like Alice in Wonderland, Amanda let Hudson open the truck door and assist her into the high seat. No, maybe not Alice. More like Cinderella in her pumpkin coach.

"You bought a truck?" Amanda asked again when

Hudson was behind the wheel, still trying to wrap her mind around the idea.

"Anything wrong with trucks?"

Bethany giggled from the small back seat, where Hudson was helping her negotiate the unfamiliar seat belt.

"What's going on here?" Amanda tried again. "Bethany? What's your daddy not telling me?"

"Not a word, Beth," Hudson said with a grin.

They drove to the far side of the lake, almost to Mooreville. Hudson acted as if he had a definite destination in mind, winding his way through the back roads of an old lake community as if he'd been here before.

When he turned onto Rosemeade Lane, Amanda got her bearings. She'd driven down this road several times, when she'd shown the Clooney mansion. She loved this part of the lake, with its huge old trees and stately homes. There was even a shady park and a small, sandy beach for swimming.

"Are we going to the park?" she asked.

But he drove right past the park.

Finally he turned into a driveway, and Amanda gave a quiet little gasp when she realized they were actually *at* the Clooney mansion. He cut the engine, opened the door, and pulled his seat forward to let Bethany out.

"Are you going to explain?"

"Just get out of the truck and come with me."

He was amused at her expense, but she was too curious now to be mad about it. She scrambled out of the truck and joined him as they walked up a wide walkway, around a fountain, and all the way up to the many-columned front porch. Lord, she'd forgotten how huge this place was.

He reached for the doorbell, then stopped. He reached into his pocket, pulled something out and handed it to her. "I almost forgot. Your key."

She looked at the gold key in her palm. "That's not my key."

"It is now!" Bethany said, giggling.

She looked again at the key, at the front door, then at Hudson. "You bought me a *house?*"

"Actually, I bought me a house. Couple of weeks ago."

"It was you?" She didn't know whether to cry with gratitude or kick him in the shins.

"I thought maybe if you could stop worrying about the bills for a while, you'd have more time for me. I didn't realize it was Mary Jo's listing."

Amanda found herself laughing. He'd bought a million-dollar house so she could spend more time with him.

"I can't accept a house from you, you know."

"Okay. For now, just accept the key. That way you can come visit us whenever you want. Of course, if you'd just marry me, the house would be yours automatically. Texas. It's a community-property state. I checked."

"You're…going…to be…here?"

"I'm certainly not going to try to drive that monster truck on those narrow Boston streets."

Amanda had never fainted in her life, but suddenly she felt as if she wanted to. Hudson took the key from her nerveless hand and opened the door, stepping aside so she could enter.

Bethany scooted inside ahead of them. "Come see

my bedroom!'' she cried, scampering across the marble-tiled foyer toward a sweeping staircase. Apparently this wasn't her first visit to the house.

"You go on ahead, honey," Hudson called after her. "We'll come upstairs in a minute."

Amanda walked to the center of the foyer and stared up at the huge chandelier.

Hudson watched her carefully. "Would you say something?"

"Please tell me this is the last secret you've been keeping from me."

"Well, there's one more."

Amanda steeled herself.

"I love you," he said. "I'm crazy, nutso in love with you. There, that's it. Everything's out in the open now."

She stopped and turned to face him, not even looking at the house. "Oh, Hudson, I love you, too. Really. But I have to ask. How rich are you?"

"Net worth at about 168 million, last I checked."

"So this house was pocket change?"

"Does that really matter? I'll give it all to charity if it bothers you. We can live in a little house and be more normal. I don't care, as long as I'm with you."

"I was going to move to Boston, you know," she said, laughing as she slowly sank to the marble floor. Her legs would no longer hold her up. "I was ready to charge up there and convert you, force you to participate in my own private twelve-step program to cure you of being a workaholic."

Hudson sat cross-legged on the floor next to her. "Would this twelve-step program have involved making love with you every night?" he said softly. "For that, I would come home early."

''That was only step one.'' She smiled and took his hand, pressing his palm against her cheek. ''You don't have to move down here. If we're going to get married, one of us has to move, but I could do it. I can sell real estate anywhere.''

''Are we? Going to get married, that is.''

''Well…''

''You're not going to think this to death, are you?''

She threw her arms around him. ''No. I mean, yes! Yes, we'll get married.''

''We'll live here, then. I've already quit my job and put my Boston houses on the market. I've talked to Ed Hardison about working at the clinic. He said they'd be happy to have a surgeon on their team, and I'd have no problem getting admitting privileges at Mother Frances. I want to live here. I want to buy our own boat.''

''A shiny, red-glitter bass boat.''

''We'll have the prettiest boat on the lake. And bicycles. We'll take off every Thursday afternoon to fish, and our blood pressure will be the envy of all our friends.''

Bethany's tennis shoes thumped against the steps as she came back downstairs. ''What are you guys doing on the floor?''

Amanda stood and dusted herself off as Hudson did the same. ''Planning our future. Our nice, long future. Now, let's go have a look at that bedroom.''

This was really turning out to be a good day, Amanda thought as she tromped up the stairs, Hudson's arm around her waist. She'd made peace with Mary Jo, Mick had learned how to turn on the vacuum cleaner, she'd gotten her dream house and she'd gotten engaged to the man who was her perfect match.

"Can we go to the drugstore later?"

"Sure. Why?"

"I want to measure my blood pressure. I'm just positive it's back to normal. How could it not be normal on a day like today?"

"We'll both measure." He paused. "Bet mine's lower."

"Hudson!"

"Kidding."

\*   \*   \*   \*   \*

*Watch for Kara Lennox's next book,*
*BOUNTY HUNTER RANSOM available in*
*February 2004*
*from Harlequin Intrigue.*

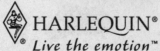

# eHARLEQUIN.com

The eHarlequin.com online community is *the* place to share opinions, thoughts and feelings!

- Joining the community is easy, fun and **FREE!**
- Connect with **other romance fans** on our message boards.
- Meet your **favorite authors** without leaving home!
- **Share opinions** on books, movies, celebrities…and *more!*

**Here's what our members say:**

"I love the friendly and helpful atmosphere filled with support and humor."
—Texanna (eHarlequin.com member)

"Is this the place for me, or what? There is nothing I love more than 'talking' books, especially with fellow readers who are reading the same ones I am."
—Jo Ann (eHarlequin.com member)

**Join today by visiting**
**www.eHarlequin.com!**

# An offer you can't afford to refuse!

**High-valued coupons for upcoming books**

**A sneak peek at Harlequin's newest line—
Harlequin Flipside™**

**Send away for a hardcover by *New York Times*
bestselling author Debbie Macomber**

### How can you get all this?

Buy four Harlequin or Silhouette books during
October–December 2003, fill out the form below and send
the form and four proofs of purchase (cash register receipts)
to the address below.

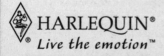

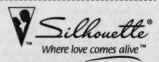

**Visit us at www.eHarlequin.com**

Q42003

○ **Your opinion is important to us!** Please take a few moments to share your thoughts with us about your experiences with Harlequin and Silhouette books. Your comments will be very useful in ensuring that we deliver books you love to read.
*Please take a few minutes to complete the questionnaire, then send it to us at the address below.*

---

Send your completed questionnaires to:
**Harlequin/Silhouette Reader Survey, P.O. Box 9046, Buffalo, NY 14269-9046**

---

1. As you may know, there are many different lines under the Harlequin and Silhouette brands. Each of the lines is listed below. Please check the box that most represents your reading habit for each line.

| Line | Currently read this line | Do not read this line | Not sure if I read this line |
|------|:---:|:---:|:---:|
| Harlequin American Romance | ❑ | ❑ | ❑ |
| Harlequin Duets | ❑ | ❑ | ❑ |
| Harlequin Romance | ❑ | ❑ | ❑ |
| Harlequin Historicals | ❑ | ❑ | ❑ |
| Harlequin Superromance | ❑ | ❑ | ❑ |
| Harlequin Intrigue | ❑ | ❑ | ❑ |
| Harlequin Presents | ❑ | ❑ | ❑ |
| Harlequin Temptation | ❑ | ❑ | ❑ |
| Harlequin Blaze | ❑ | ❑ | ❑ |
| Silhouette Special Edition | ❑ | ❑ | ❑ |
| Silhouette Romance | ❑ | ❑ | ❑ |
| Silhouette Intimate Moments | ❑ | ❑ | ❑ |
| Silhouette Desire | ❑ | ❑ | ❑ |

2. Which of the following best describes why you bought *this book?* One answer only, please.

| | | | |
|---|:---:|---|:---:|
| the picture on the cover | ❑ | the title | ❑ |
| the author | ❑ | the line is one I read often | ❑ |
| part of a miniseries | ❑ | saw an ad in another book | ❑ |
| saw an ad in a magazine/newsletter | ❑ | a friend told me about it | ❑ |
| I borrowed/was given this book | ❑ | other: _____ | ❑ |

3. Where did you buy *this book?* One answer only, please.

| | | | |
|---|:---:|---|:---:|
| at Barnes & Noble | ❑ | at a grocery store | ❑ |
| at Waldenbooks | ❑ | at a drugstore | ❑ |
| at Borders | ❑ | on eHarlequin.com Web site | ❑ |
| at another bookstore | ❑ | from another Web site | ❑ |
| at Wal-Mart | ❑ | Harlequin/Silhouette Reader | ❑ |
| at Target | ❑ | Service/through the mail | |
| at Kmart | ❑ | used books from anywhere | ❑ |
| at another department store or mass merchandiser | ❑ | I borrowed/was given this book | ❑ |

4. On average, how many Harlequin and Silhouette books do you buy at one time?

| | |
|---|:---:|
| I buy _____ books at one time | ❑ |
| I rarely buy a book | ❑ |

MRQ403HAR-1A

5. How many times per month do you shop for any *Harlequin and/or Silhouette* books?
One answer only, please.

| | | | |
|---|---|---|---|
| 1 or more times a week | ❑ | a few times per year | ❑ |
| 1 to 3 times per month | ❑ | less often than once a year | ❑ |
| 1 to 2 times every 3 months | ❑ | never | ❑ |

6. When you think of your ideal heroine, which *one* statement describes her the best?
One answer only, please.

| | | | |
|---|---|---|---|
| She's a woman who is strong-willed | ❑ | She's a desirable woman | ❑ |
| She's a woman who is needed by others | ❑ | She's a powerful woman | ❑ |
| She's a woman who is taken care of | ❑ | She's a passionate woman | ❑ |
| She's an adventurous woman | ❑ | She's a sensitive woman | ❑ |

7. The following statements describe types or genres of books that you may be
interested in reading. Pick *up to 2 types* of books that you are most interested in.

I like to read about truly romantic relationships ❑
I like to read stories that are sexy romances ❑
I like to read romantic comedies ❑
I like to read a romantic mystery/suspense ❑
I like to read about romantic adventures ❑
I like to read romance stories that involve family ❑
I like to read about a romance in times or places that I have never seen ❑
Other: _____ ❑

*The following questions help us to group your answers with those readers who are
similar to you. Your answers will remain confidential.*

8. Please record your year of birth below.

19 _____

9. What is your marital status?

single ❑    married ❑    common-law ❑    widowed ❑
divorced/separated ❑

10. Do you have children 18 years of age or younger currently living at home?

yes ❑    no ❑

11. Which of the following best describes your employment status?

employed full-time or part-time ❑    homemaker ❑    student ❑
retired ❑    unemployed ❑

12. Do you have access to the Internet from either home or work?

yes ❑    no ❑

13. Have you ever visited eHarlequin.com?

yes ❑    no ❑

14. What state do you live in?

_____

15. Are you a member of Harlequin/Silhouette Reader Service?

yes ❑    Account # _____    no ❑    MRQ403HAR-1B